A Little Night-Music

A LITTLE NIGHT-MUSIC

Discoveries in the Exploitation
of an Art

By

Gerald W. Johnson

DRAWINGS BY

RICHARD Q. YARDLEY

GREENWOOD PRESS, PUBLISHERS
WESTPORT, CONNECTICUT

To

JOHN C. BOHL

teacher of many fine flute players
and of one of the world's worst
yet who has remained
through it all
a patient and amiable gentleman
this book is inscribed
with admiration.

❁

CONTENTS

Great Men owe Fame to Promptness

FAIR WARNING

SOME unwary musician, seeing only the title of this book, may pick it up supposing it to be a treatise on his art, if not for musicians, then for intelligent and interested laymen.

It seems only fair, therefore, to display thus prominently a warning that it is not anything of the sort. The sub-title really should be taken seriously; my subject is not music, but the exploitation of music, albeit for non-commercial purposes.

Between the professional practitioner and the amateur of any art there is a great gulf fixed, but the gulf that is widest of all, I sometimes think, is the one between professional and amateur musicians. Many worthy and humane souls have endeavored to bridge it. I approve and applaud, but do not join their labors. The world is full of books written to lead the layman without musical training to a comprehension of the professional's point of view. Some of them are good, too. This is not, however, another item in that catalogue. I do not understand music myself, so I cannot instruct others in the art.

Fair Warning

But while I don't know music, I do know amateurs and this is a book about amateurs. Thus it is hardly worth a professional's attention, unless he cherishes an interest in what many of his colleagues regard as one of the most repulsive of the lower forms of life.

Even so, let him be warned, before he turns another page, that he will find herein no apologies whatever. I do not merely admit, I proclaim that I cherish no desire to do good, no ambition to contribute to the advancement of the art of music, no wish to compound ancient disputes or establish an era of brotherly love. I have no objection whatever to the existing situation and am serenely content to let amateurs and professionals continue to live in an atmosphere of mutual contempt. It is probably good for both of them.

If any musician, therefore, in the face of this warning, continues to read these pages and finds them singularly lacking in pith and sapience, incomprehensible, even, he has only himself to blame. For I sing the ruthless amateur, the loud and unabashed amateur, the irresponsible and irreverent amateur, who plays music for no good purpose, but solely to the base and sordid end of having a grand time.

On Playing the Flute Badly

ON PLAYING THE FLUTE BADLY

THE boss is really responsible for the whole thing. The boss is one of these trying people who are always bubbling with ideas and always translating their ideas into action. No doubt that is why he is the boss, but it makes him wearing on the staff. When the boss gets an idea and translates it into action, there are only two courses open to the rest of us—we can simply yes him, which is derogatory to our self-respect; or we can see his bet and raise him one, which deflates his ego and keeps him in his place and to that extent is excellent, but which is also fatiguing in most cases.

Well, some years ago the boss bought an oboe. What put the idea into his head God knows, but there it was, and something had to be done. After a couple of lessons he learned to run the C-major scale, and with that he began to get out of hand. A crisis was upon us. Were we men, or merely wage-slaves? Should we lie supine, while woodwinds triumphed over us? For the last six or eight ideas we had been yessing him continuously, and it was now clear that we had our backs to the wall;

somebody had to call him, and call him hard. And that, if you must know, is why I bought a flute.

Well, it worked. It seems that the boss had considered the flute first, but being on the wrong side of forty he had no faith in his fingers. In his mouth, on the contrary, he had sublime confidence. I make no insinuations. I merely remark that he was confident that he could achieve wonders with his mouth. But when I, who am right with him in the matter of senescence, blithely assumed the responsibility of twiddling as well as tooting, he was, as they say, struck all of a heap. He was beautifully subdued and manageable for a long time.

But that isn't the half of it. The boss and his oboe, as far as I was concerned, soon faded out of the picture. In almost no time it made no difference what happened to the oboe, or to the office, either. The matter of importance was to decide whether I got a flute, or a flute got me. Johnny B., the *maestro* who refereed the bout, had his own opinion. He thought the flute got *him*, for in an evil hour his pride betrayed him, and he announced confidently that he could teach me to play it. But presently after each round, he sat holding his head in both hands and wondering aloud why God had sent this upon him, who used to play the flute in Sousa's band. Johnny B. used to think that playing

[4]

On Playing the Flute Badly

in Sousa's band should exempt any man from the wrath of Heaven; but he was now disillusioned.

The trouble with him, of course, was that he listened to the counsel of perfection. His notion is that the only way to play a flute is to play it well, which is admirable, no doubt, in a professional musician, but made him forever incapable of comprehending, or even visualizing, my goal, which was merely to play it some way. To be sure, it would be pleasant to become a virtuoso. I should like well enough to be able to play the accompaniment for, say, Lucrezia Bori in one of these ah-ah-ah-ah-ah-ah-ah-ah pieces in which the flute is a ladder for the voice to climb. I should like to be able to show Kincaid how it ought to be done, or to play duos with Georges Barrère. It would be nice to develop the scientific side, and solve such small problems as Theobald Boehm left unfinished —for instance, to make a flute with an utterly smooth middle C and with no wolf tone in the upper F-sharp key. But I have no intention of trying to do any of these things. I am, as people go, still relatively sane—at most just a bit cracked, not completely hay-wire. Granting that no completely sane man of forty-odd would try to learn the flute, I would point out that no completely sane man has a very good time in this world; and a man may be dizzy enough to take a whirl at doing what he likes to do without imagining for a moment that he is Mahatma Gandhi, Aimee McPherson, or any other miracle-worker.

I would not willingly give the impression that Johnny B. was hypercritical. My playing, it must be admitted, did leave something to be desired, even for an amateur. We—Johnny B. and I—went in heavily for religious music, not out of piety, but because religious music is usually stately and slow, affording ample time to remember whether to grab or not to grab the G-sharp key before the next note is to be played. Consider, for example, Gounod's *Ave Maria*—I know, of course, that we musicians know that it is really the *Meditation sur le premier prelude de J. S. Bach*, but I am speaking here to the uninitiated, who call it the *Ave Maria*—well, the flute part, in Johnny B.'s opinion, should begin

"Ave Mare$^{eeee^{eee}e_{e_{e_ey}}}$aah," etc.

You see. The popular stream-line effect, a sort of curvilinear, rocking-chair motion. Whereas my own rendition is much more forthright and emphatic, usually beginning

On Playing the Flute Badly

$$e$$
$$e$$
$$e$$
$$e$$

"Ave$^{ee^{e}}$ ^{e} Mare

yah!"

which is the point at which Johnny B. used to begin rocking his head in his two hands and wondering why his Maker had it in for him.

Understand, I do not defend my individual style as a flautist. I am aware that, like the vaudeville trumpeter, all too often I blow in sweet and it comes out sour; and this must undergo some correction before even I shall be satisfied. But Johnny B., confronted with irrefutable evidence that I shall play terribly to the end of my days, was appalled, whereas I was blithely unconcerned. The point is that he is a professional and a teacher, whereas I am an amateur and interested in music only as an avocation.

And as an amateur I am convinced that what this country needs is more bum music, provided it is hand-made rather than a product of the machine age. Perfect music may be had, in these days, so easily that attaining it is no achievement at all.

A Little Night-Music

Merely by putting a record on the talking-machine and twitching a lever I can hear the *Ave Maria* played perfectly by a great artist. By twiddling the dials on the radio I can at almost any time hear a great orchestra performing marvels that are forever beyond my comprehension, not to mention my imitation. Splendid music the American people have in greater abundance than any other people ever had it before. But bad music, made by a handful of amateurs gathered in a private home, grows rarer and rarer. Why go to the considerable trouble involved in learning to play the simplest instrument when, by using the machines, you can hear the same instrument played superbly?

Why? Well, the answer depends upon what you want the music for. If it is merely to pass in at one ear and out at the other, tickling the auditory nerves and perhaps slightly roiling the emotions in its passage, then doubtless a vulcanized rubber disc or an arrangement of vacuum tubes will serve your purpose admirably. Even if listening to music is with you an intellectual exercise, a project in analysis and synthesis, with side excursions into the logic of form and development, machine-made music will serve, at least for a large part of the time.

But hand-made music serves these and yet another purpose, one with which a great many professional musicians seem totally unacquainted. It may be used as a partial substitute for and a powerful reinforcement of good liquor. You may converse with a man all an evening and still part total strangers. But you cannot play music with him, or drink with him for an evening, without learning a great deal about the way he is made. And when it comes to acting as a solvent of inhibitions and a loosener of reflexes, one drink, combined with a lot of hand-made music, is far more effective than ten drinks while you listen to a talking-machine or a radio.

In these United States of America this is an especially important matter. We have abandoned the compounds of nitroglycerine and corrosive sublimate that were our tipple for thirteen years and have applied ourselves again to beverages approved by civilized men. But if the nation, while the fit of common sense is on it, could carry the policy one step further and fortify its liquor with strong music, it could remain beautifully tight on a tenth of the liquor otherwise required, to the profit both of its stomach and of its purse. But the good music the machines provide is only so much tea—it cheers but doesn't inebriate. It takes the bad music you play yourself to send you reeling and happy to bed.

Another noble experiment which the propagation of bad music—meaning music badly played in the home—might advance is that of debunking the American's attitude toward the art. The American, especially in the small towns and rural districts, has gone farther than any other man toward establishing a false and vicious association between good composers and tail coats. Opera means eight dollars a seat, a white tie, and boredom. Symphonic programs mean five dollars only, but they also include a white tie and boredom. So when he hears Bach, Beethoven, and Brahms, or, for that matter, Tschaikowsky, Rimsky-Korsakoff, Stravinsky, or Prokovieff, the American, even if he doesn't array his body in tails, dresses his mind in a sheet-iron shirt and prepares to endure heroically in behalf of Culture.

This is not altogether bad. A respectful attitude toward the giants accords with public decorum, which is not to be decried. But the musical experience of the average American oscillates between Bach and Tin-Pan Alley, and this is not so good. The experience of other countries indicates that the real delight of the great masses of people lies somewhere between swallow-tail music and shirt-tail music, and a man who is bored by the Second Symphony of Brahms may also be bored by the Livery Stable Blues and still be capable of relishing certain forms of music. Now when half a dozen people go to the trouble of assembling at the house of one of them, lugging instruments with them, it is a hundred to one that they will not waste much time on the products of Tin-Pan Alley and, if they are really amateurs, it is equally certain that they cannot encompass the mightier works of the mightiest musicians. So they are driven perforce into the company of a set of men who are not august enough to inspire awe, but are nevertheless men of a type with whom it would be well for Americans to have much more commerce—sprightly men, intelligent, witty, urbane, sophisticated, with an occasional flash of genius, but, above all, eternally entertaining and amusing men.

I can think of nothing that American life needs worse than suave intelligence, coupled with good-humor and a real, but not solemn, appreciation of excellence in the arts. And for this reason I think an American is a better American if he has tried to play a little Offenbach, a little Bizet, and Meyerbeer, and Rossini, and Mendelssohn, maybe a *very* little Verdi, a touch of Balfe and a *soupçon* of de Koven, and, of course, unlimited quantities of

[11]

A Little Night-Music

Johann Strauss. These lads may not have been titans under whose tread the earth shook. But they were considerably smarter than you and I, at that, as we speedily find out when we try to unravel their work. They may be understood by any man of average intelligence, but not so easily that he feels ridiculous for having taken them seriously. They may be played, after a fashion, by a pretty poor musician, but to bring out all that is in them calls, not for a skip-jack, but for a battle cruiser. Don't worry—you will never get so good that Johann Strauss will have no new beauties for you to reveal. When the tallest boys in the trade, people of the stature of Kreisler, Stokowski, Paderewski, Casals, and the like have never exhausted this type of music, you and I are not going to do so. We can play it until palsy intervenes without wearing it out. But it does do this: no minor master ever quits by walking off the stage with his hands by his side; always, with a bow and a sweeping gesture, he indicates a greater one to follow. Being gentlemen, they know their betters, and promptly and gladly yield precedence to them. If you play Bizet for a while, you can listen to Bach without a white tie choking your soul or an armor-plated shirt protecting your mind.

This, though, is by the way. The real reason

On Playing the Flute Badly

for playing fine music even though you play badly, is simply that you have a grand time doing it. Among other things, by this method you soon find out which musicians among your acquaintances are artists and which are merely arty. The arty kind will never lend a hand in a performance pretty sure to lead to the murder of some respectable composer. They are too solemn to risk being human. But your artist, knowing that the striving after an unattainable perfection is what gives validity to any art, respects the striving, even when it falls far short of attainable excellence. And there are few more fruitful and delightful contacts to be made in this world than that with a fine musician come down off his high horse and joining with a bunch of amateurs in a murderous assault on some masterpiece.

There is a charming story told of the most learned musician of my acquaintance, a man whose musical scholarship has gained him an international reputation, but whose favorite relaxation is to join, once a week, a group including various lawyers, doctors, architects, editors and merchants in attacks on various celebrities, not excluding Beethoven, Brahms, or Bach. Back in the days when beer was still homebrew, not yet reduced to a mere commercial efficiency, this crew had set down their seidels and were furiously engaged in the assault, when they were dumfounded by the learned musician's playing a run which wasn't there. For this man to make a mistake in reading music was as if Einstein had said twice six is ten, or as if Professor Piccard's head had begun to swim as he mounted a step-ladder. It was simply inconceivable; yet it had happened. But then a spectator, sitting at the musician's side, began to roar and the truth came out. A fly had lighted on the music, just athwart the lowest line of the staff, and had walked quickly up across it. And the home-brew had been so good that the learned musician had promptly played the fly, *maestoso*.

For my part, I regard the incident of the fly as better proof that this man has served the art of music well than I do all his labors in musty and obscure libraries, sweating over dusty manuscripts of medieval chants, or his acquaintance with the folk-songs of Iraq or the notation employed at the time of the Crusades. For he is strengthening in his city the popular realization that music must be included in any life if it is to be a gracious, spacious and well-ordered life. He assists at the creation of a great deal of bum music; but he also assists the creation for his art of love, respect, and appreciation. And this is service indeed.

On Playing the Flute Badly

So I broached to Johnny B. the subject of this chapter—the idea that here is a nation of 123,000,-000 people with not enough bum music. "There is something in it," said Johnny B., assuming a judicial air. "That is to say, there was something in it a short time ago. But now that you have taken up the flute, I think the balance is redressed."

A Little Night-Music

A LITTLE NIGHT-MUSIC

WHEN I was a boy it was part of the destiny of the American female child to spend countless hours incarcerated in the parlor, pounding the piano. This torture was inflicted with as calm an indifference to the feelings of the victim as was the binding of the feet of the Chinese female child, and for the same purpose—to increase her social prestige when she grew up. For in those days the music intended to smooth the ways when a party was launched had to be handmade, and the girl who was not competent to assist in its making was socially disabled.

Today that is no longer true. With all that has been said about the effect of the talking-machine and the radio on the art of music, almost no attention has been paid to their influence on the emancipation of women, or at least of little girls from what was frequently drudgery of an appalling type. The child with no real liking for music who, nevertheless, had to learn to play the piano was a truly pitiable figure, and her release is no inconsiderable triumph of modern science.

A Little Night-Music

At the same time this freedom was bought at a price which many musicians and social philosophers have denounced as too high. For one thing, it has played hob with the piano industry. For another, it has made teaching music ever more precarious as a means of livelihood. But the gravest charge against mechanical music is that it tends to separate the art still farther from the lives of the American people, making it a mere accessory to other pleasures, not much more significant in itself than the wax that smooths the floor for dancers. People began to foresee the time when the practice of music would be confined to a handful of highly skilled professionals, playing in broadcasting studios or before recording apparatus in talking-machine factories.

I confess that for some years I was one who entertained this view, forgetting that the mere fact that it is logical is pretty good evidence that it is false. For in this illogical world that which is patently inevitable practically never happens. It is true that there are now thousands of middle-class homes without a piano—a condition unimaginable in my youth. It is true that it is much more difficult to make a living by teaching music than it was thirty years ago. It is true that music as an "accomplishment" is no longer necessarily part of the education of every young woman of good family. But that all this has had any bad effect on music as an art remains to be proved. My reasons for doubting it are, I confess, highly particular; but that they fairly represent the general I have no doubt whatever.

It comes from having listened recently, for the second time, to Mozart's *Eine Kleine Nachtmusik* played by a competent orchestra. A year or two earlier I had heard the string section of the Boston Symphony Orchestra play it, with Koussevitsky conducting. Needless to say, it was superbly done. Not long ago I heard it again. This time the orchestra was composed of students in a music conservatory. Their performance was not to be compared with that of the great professional orchestra of course; but it had an effect on me that the Bostonians never approached. As far as I was concerned, the first performance was entertainment—of a very superior order, to be sure, but merely entertainment, whereas the latter, for reasons that I hope to set out, and perhaps to make clear, was music.

It is all based on half a dozen brutal, nay, murderous, assaults on the blameless Mozart. These were not grudge fights. Nobody had anything against the composer. On the contrary, he was

murdered with the greatest respect and in a spirit
of high idealism—as a matter of fact, in pursuance
of a program of popular education. If there is anything that is beyond peradventure soundly American, it is the principle that any sort of crime may
be committed with impunity if it is done in pursuance of a program of popular education. The
idea in this case was to encourage children with
musical talent by giving them an opportunity to
put their music lessons to some use; to this end
small neighborhood ensembles were to be organized throughout the city, in which parents would
play with their children. I still think that, like the
notion of repatriating American Negroes in Li-
beria, it was a grand idea, even if it hasn't worked
out exactly as it was intended to work.

Our own ensemble, in pursuance of this plan,
chose to attack *Eine Kleine Nachtmusik.* I don't
know why. It wasn't my idea, because, while this
work is one of Mozart's lighter efforts, it is still
Mozart, which means that there is a lot in it which
is going to make the average amateur musician
perspire profusely before he produces anything like
what the composer intended. My own vote was
cast in favor of "The Sunshine of Your Smile."
Now there is an opus that offers a musician of my
capacity a chance to shine. It is almost the equal

of a good, sound hymn tune in the number of opportunities it offers for lingering, languishing,
dying-duck effects, whereas this swift, bright,
sinewy music of Mozart's ruthlessly demands attention to business. However, I was overruled, and
Mozart it was.

Our ensemble, you observe, was organized
originally for children. It consists, at present, of a
psychoanalyst, an M.D., a dentist, a kindergarten
teacher, a housewife, a newspaper man, three little
girls, and a woman who shows up strangely in
this gallery, for she is a professional violinist. The
average age of the members must be well up in
the thirties. The main function of the three little
girls so far is to demonstrate to the others how
the third-violin part may be played demurely and
dutifully, just as it was written. The function of
the professional is somewhat indeterminate; in the
beginning it was believed that she was to act as
director; but that was before the strength of character of our group was demonstrated. We are
bold, determined people. We will not be put upon.
In the first place we add a couple of flutes and a
piano to play music written for strings alone; and
in the second place we play with a single-minded
resolution known only to amateurs of the most
extreme type, altogether foreign to professionals.

If the flutes, for example, finish a movement and quit three measures ahead of everyone else, why that only goes to show their superior speed and endurance. Thus the energies of the professional have been almost entirely consumed in incessantly biting off her words; for she is grimly determined, even under the most extreme provocation, to remember that she is a lady.

Of all her original aspirations for the ensemble, Charity—her real name isn't Charity, but call her that, because she suffereth long and is kind—retains only one. In the second movement of *Eine Kleine Nachtmusik* Mozart wrote seven and a half measures and then put in a repeat sign, meaning go back to the beginning and play it over again. If you will observe closely, you will see Charity at about the sixth measure beginning to draw a long breath, which she discharges on the second beat of the eighth measure in a wild shout of "Repeat!" Some day, some sweet if distant day, she is confident, every instrument without exception will revert to the beginning, instead of playing the rest of that eighth measure before it can be stopped. It may never happen, but at any rate it is something to look forward to; and what is life without something to look forward to?

Careful study of the foregoing may lead you to

understand why it is that our ensemble plays in strict privacy; but it may leave you still bemused as to why it plays at all. Obviously, love of music alone is not the explanation, for every house in the block can be, and is filled with better music every time some one twists the dial of the radio. Personal vanity is not the motive, since we permit no audiences and have no present ambition to appear in public. Parental interest is not all of it, because two of the three children present are sent by parents who do not play. I dismiss with contempt the canard that our real motive is to beat down real estate values in our neighborhood; but to make the real motive plain is neither simple nor easy.

For ensemble-playing, if the music is really worth while, is work. We have been struggling for an hour and a half, and things have come to a halt while Charity explains for the eightieth time exactly where a certain *decrescendo* ought to begin. She lays aside the ruler she has been using for a baton and borrows a pencil to mark the place on the various parts. I lay the flute on my knees and gently pinch my lip, trying to restore the circulation, while the psychoanalyst beside me alternately bends and straightens his arms, for the same purpose. We look over the music-stand at Charity—

a harassed woman if ever there was one. Ygg, the kindergartner—her real name isn't Yggdrasil, either, but as pianist she supports the whole works, so it is as appropriate as Charity—Ygg puts her hands down flat on the piano-bench beside her, and gently shifts her weight from one to the other; after a hard day's work she has come miles to be here. The dentist and the M.D. sigh in unison and tighten a peg each on their violins. The housewife, flushed, shifts her 'cello slightly and drags back the hair that has fallen down over her face during the last rapid passage. Only the three little girls sit properly in their places and listen gravely while Charity lectures. Iron women, they—ah, youth, youth. . . .

Not one of us belongs to the army of the unemployed. Each of us has done a day's labor at one task or another. Even the children have been in school. What are we doing here, now that night has fallen, working even harder than we did all day? Playing Mozart? Bah! I remember, ruefully, that the time is one hundred and thirty-two beats to the minute and that just ahead lies a staccato run of two measures and a half in sixteenth notes, spattered with accidentals from end to end. When I hit that I shall blow up. I always do. Apparently I always shall. It seems to be a case of what Gilbert called "weakness of intellects." I know how it should be played; I can play it, in fact, have played it time and again in practice, but there is a hex upon me and when I hit it I shall blow up. Is that playing Mozart? Again, bah!

But consider this: I am a newspaper man, not a musician, and during the impending wrestling bout that staccato run is as certain to get the best of me as the angel was to put Jacob out of business at Peniel. Nevertheless, so long as the hopeless contest rages I shall in no wise trouble my head about whether the Administration is spending four millions or four billions or four trillions, nor about the Far Eastern situation, nor about the menaces of Fascism and Communism. Over there the dentist and the M.D., as they desperately struggle to attain a high E flat simultaneously, will give no heed to caries or appendectomies or the grisly specter of state medicine. Mozart will drive Montessori out of Ygg's head, and soap, servants, and darning-cotton out of the housewife's; and the psychoanalyst will worry over no inhibitions and reaction-times save those that affect his own fingers.

What Charity gets out of it I don't know. She has worked all day in a great conservatory where music is served with a skill and singleness of purpose foreign to our group; so to spend the evening playing music is a busman's holiday for her. But Charity is more than a musician exclusively; she is gifted with humor and with curiosity about life as well as tone. No doubt with us she sees and hears things that never happen in the conservatory, and that she probably never imagined could happen anywhere. Sometimes I am inclined to suspect that Charity may be learning more than any of us; only she is much too polite to say what it is.

That, though, is speculation. What I know, beyond peradventure, is that when we have played from eight to ten, and the dismembered fragments of poor Mozart are scattered to the four winds, those of us who are not musicians come back to the affairs of our ordinary lives a trifle confused and uncertain, as one who says, "Well, let's see now, where were we?" We have stepped out of our ordinary lives. We have divested ourselves for two hours of our ordinary emotions, anxieties, and perplexities. Our very lack of skill insures this. Were we all highly skilled musicians we might— although I doubt it—play *Eine Kleine Nachtmusik* with half our minds still engaged in reviewing the follies, failures, and futilities of the preceding hours of daylight; but as it is, it takes all our mental resources to grapple successfully with the problem of just when Charity is going to shout "Repeat!" Not a brain cell is left to harbor the corroding worries of the working-day.

This is enough to justify our labors, but it is by no means all. Even in our ensemble minor miracles occur now and then. Not an evening do we play together without playing a few measures correctly. And the delighted surprise that this occasions is an emotional experience denied to real musicians. They may feel the delight, but it is not accentuated by surprise: that is vouchsafed the amateur in compensation for his low estate. Granted that it usually lasts for a matter of seconds, rather than minutes, that instant is great when the clamor suddenly and inexplicably resolves itself into order, form, and beauty. It is infinitely greater than perfect music which you hear sitting in the audience at a concert, for you are a part of it. This instrument in your hands, this inanimate thing of lifeless wood and metal, by your agency has suddenly come alive, has become one of these strong voices singing together. Then you play a D sharp instead of the D that was called for and the miracle vanishes. But it has happened; for a moment the thick veil of your own ineptitude has been whisked aside and you have had a flashing glimpse of the splendor that might be. And is there a kick in it? Now, I ask you!

But even if this happened more rarely than it does, there would remain one powerful reason, aside from the pursuance of a program of popular education, to induce our ensemble to continue its labors. The best reason for the existence of an amateur organization of this sort is not that its members may play music, but that they may hear music in some other than the physiological sense. Set up vibrations in the air at the rate of four hundred and forty a second, and a physicist, a Deems Taylor, a Hottentot, you and I, and a trained seal will all hear the A above middle C; but to assume that we all hear the same thing is to assume too much—very much too much. For hearing does not consist solely of the sensations conveyed by the auditory nerves to certain brain cells—that is to say, while it may do so to a physiologist, it doesn't to you and me and a trained seal. To us, hearing involves not only the auditory sensations themselves, but also their associations; and the associations you and I attach to sounds are, I trust, different from those attached to them by the seal.

I venture to doubt that any amount of training makes much difference in one's emotional response to music, which is, after all, the factor that separates genuine musicians from the rest of the world. Every concertgoer has learned that it is possible for a man to attain an amazing technical competence without much emotional response; but such players never reach the top flight. They may become startling virtuosi, but not great musicians.

But for the ordinary amateur, whose emotional response is sufficiently great to make him enjoy music, but not enough to make him a musician, laboring at some master-work enormously enriches his experience in hearing it, because it gives him a new appreciation of excellence. And what is an educated, a cultivated, a civilized man if not one who has a keen appreciation of excellence in many fields?

The man who never sat behind the wheel of a motor-car may think he knows what good driving is, but he doesn't; and he who never sat under a conductor's baton has not much better comprehension of what really fine ensemble playing is. The baton need not be Stokowski's or Toscanini's. For the amateur with any imagination the equivalent of Charity's ruler will serve excellently. I know —did I not sit and listen to *Eine Kleine Nachtmusik* the other night?

When I heard it before, with Koussevitsky con-

ducting, I went along as a mere hitch-hiker, so to
speak, totally ignorant of the road, and with only
a tourist's mild interest in its loops and curves,
hairpin turns, long climbs toward a shining sky,
and breath-taking swoops down into the depths.
But this time I knew it well. At least half a dozen
times in the previous three months our ensemble
had started out bravely and jauntily on that tempt-
ing highroad. What matter that we had frequently,
not to say invariably, piled into the ditch ere long?
What matter that we practically never took one
of its dizzy curves without running off onto the
shoulder, hitting a few projecting rocks and roots,
and rattling and careening horribly before we
swung back to the smooth surface again? That
simply meant that we could appreciate the excellence of a really competent performance.

And did we ride! There is not much music more
gay and jocund than the opening movement of this
work. The semicircle of shining instruments and
white shirtfronts, punctuated by the conductor's
straight black back like an exclamation point in
the middle; the expectant hush over the house;
the pause with the baton raised vertically, motion-
less; its swift downward swoop, the instant burst
of sound, and the sudden awed, incredulous realiza-

tion that they had hit it, yes, by George, they hit it all together and all on the key—what a moment!

And then to ride with an expert driver handling a splendid machine along a way that one has traveled over and over again, laboriously and precariously—to travel at ease and yet recognizing every rise and fall, every twist and turn, knowing intimately and inwardly applauding every danger skillfully avoided, every curve dextrously rounded, is well worth all our evenings' labors. Here now the orchestra is well into it; here is that *sforzando* where the flutes blew out a gasket last Saturday night—they have taken it at forty-five miles an hour and without a quiver. There is that *crescendo* rising to a high whole note where the 'cello threw a tire the time before that—with a swoop and a triumphant scream from twenty strings they are over it and gone. Now they are approaching that hairpin turn where the second fiddle forgot that the key was G and played four F naturals in quick succession, and poor Charity had to be dragged out of the wreck and fanned with a towel to bring her to. No such disaster is thinkable with this powerful racer. Finale; and they bring up with a fine, smooth flourish without a jar or a squeal from the brakes.

The first movement, the allegro, of *Eine Kleine*

A Little Night-Music

Nachtmusik is followed by a romance, marked andante, that is as soft and sensuous as the first was bright and crystalline. Here Mozart let himself go. It is easy to fabricate program notes for this incomparable serenade; indeed, it is almost impossible not to believe that the jaunty, laughing allegro was to awaken the beloved, the minuet to entertain her, and the rondo to bid her a gay good-night. Which means, of course, that the aim and object of the whole was to form a perfect setting for the love song that is the romance. And when Mozart set himself to write a love song, he didn't write merely "Affectionately yours," and let it go at that. He starts with two short notes like a sob in the throat and then breaks into a long, wavering cry that is at once an avowal, a paean of praise and triumph, and a passionate appeal, and which sinks again into crooning tenderness. And this theme he embroiders endlessly, constantly adding to its richness and magnificence, turning back again and again to emphasize it by restatement, but never for an instant concealing or disguising the flaming passion that is at its heart.

Leaning over to say so to Charity, sitting next to me, I inadvertently touched her shoulder, whereupon she started out of her reverie and automatically snapped, "Repeat!" But the orchestra had already begun to do so—all of them at the same time—so I altered my comment. I said that I judged this music, on the whole, to be unfit for a Sunday-school picnic; and she said, "Decidedly so," and sank into reverie again.

But for once I understood a musician at a concert, at least in part. I had attended concerts with musicians before that, and I was aware, of course, that they were hearing things in the pattern of tone that were far beyond my duller ears and untrained understanding. That is still true and will always be true of course, since I possess neither the auditory mechanism nor the emotional temperament that go to make a musician. But whereas before our ensemble started its murderous career, a musician listening to Mozart's serenade would have seemed to me like a Chinaman listening to Chinese, today he is like a Frenchman listening to French; the point being that I know not a word of Chinese, but understand French as well as I understand music—that is to say, well enough to know that I am missing nine-tenths of a great language, and to envy the fellow who is getting it all.

You may reasonably infer that this is maddening, and you will be quite right. But isn't it just the things that madden us that fill us with awareness of being alive? The goal that is in sight but beyond our reach is our torture, but also our deep delight.

If it is not so, then all I can say is that there is evidently a touch of insanity affecting our group; for I am quite sure that the best machine, not merely that a radio engineer ever built, but that one ever imagined, would not dissuade us from toiling on toward a goal that we shall never reach. The radio very efficiently supplies all the party music necessary; thus it has released from the necessity of learning music those thousands of people whose real interest is in the party, not in the music. This obvious boon to parties has worked to the damage of music as a profession; but it may be plausibly argued that it has worked to the advantage of music as an art by drawing away from it people who are not interested in it as an art, but only as an adjunct to social gaieties.

And those who remain faithful are unshakable in their devotion. I do not mean the born musicians, to whom music is life, but such amateurs as we are. Nothing can deter us, because our motive is low. It is not the praiseworthy motive that drives many people to suffer through innumerable classical concerts, to wit, the acquisition of culture. It is not the altruistic motive of contributing to the pleasure of others by playing while they dance. Still less is it the pious motive of enriching and adorning religious services. Our motive is nothing more than the unexalted desire to have a grand time. But this is the most durable of all motives; there is not the least reason to fear that mechanized music will have any effect on it.

And if we are slightly insane, we have plenty of company. For my part, I believe that within the past five years the remnants of the population to whom making music is infinitely more fun than listening to the radio are beginning to draw together. I know that the number of neighborhood ensembles in our town today is greater than it has been at any time since the advent of mechanized music scattered those that existed twenty years ago; and although the number of amateur players is smaller than it was in the old days, I believe that their interest is more sincere and, therefore, more likely to be permanent.

And I suspect that they are playing, or will soon be playing, better music than they played in the old days, when the real interest of half their number was in something outside the music itself. In this I am once more arguing from the particular to the general, which is dangerous, but not necessarily wrong. For I know what it means to hear played superbly something that you have been playing badly; I know that it means, among other things, getting five times as much fun for the price of your concert ticket as you used to get. So I am glad, after all, that we took up Mozart instead of sticking to tunes that I can play; for I have heard *Eine Kleine Nachtmusik* played well, and am likely to hear it again, whereas I consider quite remote the chance that Koussevitsky will ever put "The Sunshine of Your Smile" on one of his programs.

The Art of Coming In

THE ART OF COMING IN

THE title on the cover is impressive, as the covers of most German editions of music are. Printed in that type which resembles black-letter, *Zweite Sinfonie von Jos. Haydn* looks stern, serious, learned. Here, says the amateur musician confronted with it, is the sort of music that real musicians play; no red or blue ink; no half-tone photographs of vaudeville or operatic stars; no harvest moons, or log cabins, or scrolls, flowers, and curlicues; not even an English title. Let low fellows whose ambition reaches nothing higher than playing dance music delight in gaudy covers, if they will; here is the sort of stuff the conservatory students lug about in their briefcases; this belongs to the Higher Things of Life; this, in brief, is the real McCoy.

And so, no doubt, it is, taken as a whole. Not great, to be sure, in the sense that the *Eroica* is great, old Papa Haydn's Second Symphony nevertheless is cool, clear, delightful music, with quite enough substance in it to permit a fine player to show what he can do. Oh no, it is not to be sniffed at, by any means—taken as a whole.

But what amateur player ever took it as a whole?
What amateur, if he is a real, blown-in-the-bottle,
incorrigible amateur, ever took anything written
for ensemble-playing as a whole? When he ac-
quires the habit of hearing the ensemble as a unit
and thinking of it as a unit, he begins to be good,
which means that he is beginning, as a musician,
to edge away from the amateur and over toward
the professional side. It is characteristic of your
ravening amateur that he thinks of the Second
Symphony, or of any other music, as consisting of
the part written for his instrument plus some
trimmings supplied by other members of the
group. This I take to be the fundamental principle,
the very mud-sill of amateurishness, without which
it cannot exist in its true character.

And viewed from this angle, Haydn's Second
Symphony, I must say, is open to serious criticism.
Take, as evidence, the flute part. Now any amateur flautist knows that the ideal symphony would
consist, not of continuous music for the flute—
that is a libel upon us flautists invented by scornful string players—but of music broken by judi-
ciously placed rests coming, by preference, after
each rapid run and lasting not more than three
measures, or five at the outside. Just to show that
I am not bigoted, I will even go so far as to say

that advantage might be taken of these rests to insert some good solos for the other instruments —provided, of course, that the best are reserved for the flute. The *Zweite Sinfonie von Jos. Haydn,* I regret to say, does not measure up to this standard at all. On the contrary, as I stare disconsolately at the flute part it seems to consist of a few oases of music strewed thinly over a desert of thick black bars, with numerals over them—rests, damnably long rests, during which the flute is out of action altogether. Would you have believed it, of as judicious and sensible a man as Haydn?

However, composers are like that, and one must take the music as it is written and make what one can of it. Our ensemble, therefore, assailed Haydn with a vigor worthy of producing better results. Charity, indeed, distinguished herself. She proved that she really ought to be appointed to some high office under the Roosevelt administration, that is, if the President is sincere in his early announcement that he wants people around him who can take it. For Charity unquestionably can take it. She played with us from the start, and kept coming, which gives her a just claim to be called, if she had no other distinction, the most durable violinist on the Atlantic seaboard. At the end of every session she was wild-eyed and her voice had been reduced to a croak and occasionally she had to be assisted from the room; but never, not even once, did she pass out completely in the midst of a performance. True, there was a moment one evening when I thought she was gone; the passage under dissection had a repeat sign at the end; the ensemble bore down on it at high speed and when it was reached every instrument—I repeat, *every* one—whipped back to the beginning and started again, correctly. The surprise almost did what all the atrocities of the previous season had not accomplished. Charity reeled. She recovered in a second or two, and went on, but it was a near thing, a very near thing.

However, as the season wore on and Haydn's Second Symphony was hammered flatter and flatter, it was being borne in upon me that perhaps the old man's deplorable extravagance with rests for the flute might be turned to good account by an aspiring amateur. At least it afforded practice in the great art of Coming In.

It is an art that I do not care to practice. It is an art that is abhorrent to me. It is the most pedestrian, the most utilitarian, of all the arts. But it is, unfortunately, also among the most useful. For the man who can rest for seventy-four measures, as this Haydn expects the flutes to do in one place, and then come in correctly on the up beat of the seventy-fifth, is a man of high and estimable qualities. Consider the list of mental accomplishments this feat requires. In the first place, he who can do it has learned to concentrate. In the second place, he has developed mental tenacity, for seventy-four measures last a long time. In the third place, he has precision, or he will never come in on that last beat. Finally, this particular piece of music demands not only that he come in at this juncture, but that he come in *forte*, and this demands a self-confidence unsurpassed by that either of Professor Rexford Guy Tugwell or of General Hugh S. Johnson. It is one thing to come in *pianissimo*, to sneak in, as it were, furtively and tentatively, with the hope of backing out hastily before anyone discovers you are there, if it proves to be the wrong moment; but it is another thing altogether to enter with a blare that will create a loud and hideous discord if you are not on the dot. That takes magnificent assurance. But a man whose mental endowment includes concentration, tenacity, precision, and self-confidence is a man of no trifling attainments. He commands respectful consideration.

No doubt it is possible for the educated musician to develop these qualities sufficiently for the purpose of his profession without necessarily developing them as regards any other aspect of life. But what of it? The traits characteristic of educated musicians have no imaginable application to our ensemble. Besides, what is music for if not to quicken one's perception and appreciation of the ideal? The amateur may be debarred by his own small skill from ever producing ideal music; should he not, then, be the more eager to console himself with such high philosophical matters as the noises he produces may suggest to him? If he can't kid himself into believing he will ever learn to play, maybe he can kid himself into believing he can learn to philosophize.

Look you, then, how development of the art of coming in may be profitable, if not to the children of light, at least to the children of this world. Niccolo Machiavelli, Balthasar Gracian, Michel Eyquem de Montaigne never invented a better allegory by which to illustrate the art of worldly wisdom; for the elements of that complex effect we call success are here. All of these sages, for example, command imperturbability in the face of imminent mischances. I defy anyone to devise better training in that quality than to practice remaining impassive during the last three or four bars of a nineteen-measure rest while four, or six, or ten instruments in the hands of raging amateurs are tearing down the homestretch, galloping raggedly upon the point where you must suddenly strike a high note that will cut through the rest of the noise like a knife through cheese.

Again, all three recommend intellectual self-sufficiency, a bland, firm disregard of the opinions of all others, once you have made up your mind you are right. Would you develop that obviously valuable quality? Then try counting to yourself *"seventeen*-two-three-four," while the man at your elbow, whose rest began at a different point, is chanting *"eleven*-two-three-four" with all the certainty, assurance, and weight of authority of Father Coughlin at the microphone. If at the next down beat you can say "eighteen" and not "twelve," then, indeed, you are making progress. That admirable commentator on the sociological implications of amateur music, Catharine Drinker Bowen, reports the case of a little girl who skillfully evaded this particular difficulty by always counting an andante movement with her stomach, but that is a strange, incomprehensible idea to me, to be classed with the spiritual exercises of the Hindu mystics, who, says the *Bengal Lancer*, seek communion with the Absolute by visceral agitation. It sounds all right, but I don't know how she does it.

They all recommend cultivation of an equanimity that is proof against either defeat or triumph. This is essential to the art of coming in, as I know by sad experience, both ways. Coming in wrong, especially on a loud and brilliant note, is one of those experiences which have, fortunately, few parallels in polite society. Not Cortez on a peak in Darien, not Robinson Crusoe ere the advent of Friday, not the man who voted for Landon in 1936 was so terribly alone as the player who comes in ahead of the beat. Yet for the incorrigible amateur, alas! there is danger in being right; for the amateur who comes in solo, squarely and truly, clearly and cleanly, right on the pitch and right on the beat, in his astonishment is likely to miss the next two notes altogether. Equanimity—ah, there is an ideal!

They all recommend the maintenance of a healthy skepticism, not to say cynicism, with regard to your fellow man. "Put not your trust in princes," warned Solomon, and if he had been a flute-player he might have added, "nor yet in pianists, fiddlers, oboists, trumpeters, or drums." It is all very well to take a pencil and sketch in, where you have a long rest, two or three measures of the violin part to cue you in; but he is an impractical idealist who assumes as a matter of course that the fiddlers are going to play the music when they get to it, or play it so that it is recognizable. As a matter of fact, undue trustfulness does not survive any length of experience in an amateur ensemble. Colleagues are always hopeless. I have never yet encountered a hard-bitten, battle-scarred amateur who would trust his colleagues to play three successive measures in the same key, not to mention the same tempo. A calm anticipation of the worst is their characteristic attitude; which is a trait approved by all the experts on worldly wisdom.

In brief, what is success if not having the ability, or the luck, to come in exactly right? Skim the pages of history and note how many giants stand out in the memory of mankind for having hit the big bass drum at precisely the proper moment. Blücher is immortal among captains because he came in squarely on the beat at Waterloo. Doubtless he was a good soldier before that, and doubtless he was a good one afterward; but what does it matter? When the last movement of the Napoleonic symphony was being played, after that dramatic pause when Wellington and Napoleon both rested, he crashed in with the first measure of the roaring finale. And, as far as history is concerned, that's Blücher. It may be that the greatness of Stonewall Jackson is best measured by the fact that military historians are still puzzling over how he could have missed his cue at Seven Pines. An astonishing number of explanations have been advanced, for almost any theory seems less fantastic than to assume that Stonewall counted wrong, even once.

For those of us who can never do it right, there is mortification of the spirit in reading of the great men who owe fame and fortune to a prompt and effective entrance. Suppose Cæsar had crossed the Rubicon one thirty-second behind the beat, what sort of impression would he have made on history? His great threat would have been altogether in his own imagination, and he would have been no more effective than an earlier Dr. Wirt. Or if at Chicago in 1932, when the drums and trumpets of the nominating convention ceased and Franklin D. Roosevelt started that enthralling solo that swept the country, suppose he had failed to realize that the key had shifted to Wet Major, what a mess he would have made of it! What a mess his opponent did make of it by failing to note in time the modulation that was going on!

Such reflections tend to sadden and subdue the

amateur player. If Waterloo was won on the playing-fields of Eton and Harrow, who knows what battles and campaigns may have been lost behind a music-rack? Is this incapacity to come in properly the imprimatur, the sign manual of some profound and ineradicable defect in character and intelligence? In the second movement of the Haydn symphony is a flute solo beginning with a B-flat, shooting up to a high D and down again to a G —a nice, clear, emphatic bit, in which the flute restates, with the silvery clarity of which it alone is capable, that which the whole orchestra has just been shouting. At least that is what Haydn meant to be done, and what Mr. Barrère and Mr. Kincaid do. At that point opportunity knocks at the flautist's door; and when, at that point, there arises from my flute not the faëry voice of Prospero's Ariel, working strong magic, but the quavering voice of the most decrepit beldame among Macbeth's witches, magical indeed, but only to convert the Second Symphony into a blasted heath, is this a portent for him who can rede it, does this explain to a philosopher why it is that I am no Roosevelt? Horrid thought!

But it has an antidote. Mastery of the art of coming in may mark the successful man, but, after all, not all successful men are admirable. Let us

122908

consider the consolation of the sour grapes. Search history as you will, you will find no more complete masters of the art than in that celebrated pair, the Duke of Otranto, better known as Fouché, and the Prince of Beneveto, better known as Talleyrand. Starting under Louis XVI, these played through perhaps the most difficult political program ever presented—the Monarchy, the Revolution, the Empire, the Restoration, and the Revolution of July. Throughout, neither of them ever missed a cue, ever was a split second before or behind the beat, ever got off the key for an instant, ever accelerated or retarded the tempo. Both were hugely successful, both died loaded with riches and honors. Still, at the time of their last conspicuous appearance, when they came in together, exactly right, as usual, a certain Chateaubriand wrote a program note which is remembered better than the duet. Observing lame Talleyrand leaning on the arm of Fouché, he said, "I seemed to see Vice advancing, supported by Crime." Now, you fellows who can always do it exactly right, take that!

After all, there are some of us who would rather have been Henry Clay than Talleyrand, yet Clay, in the great symphony of world affairs, was a conspicuous example of those who never master the art of coming in. He assailed the Bank ahead of the baton, and he defended the Bank behind it. He feared Andrew Jackson in 1819, when Old Hickory was not dangerous, and scorned him in 1824, when he was deadly. He rejected appointive office when it was his cue to take it, and he accepted it from Adams when he should have refused. Sometimes he may have been right, but he never was President. And a century later even Clay's ability to strike the right note at the wrong time was excelled by that of William Jennings Bryan. He played bi-metallism in 1896, whereas that measure wasn't written in the score until 1933; he played anti-imperalism in 1900, whereas the rest of the national orchestra is only just now approaching it; in 1908 he essayed a solo on the Money Devil theme, whereas that part really belongs to Senator Glass, who rendered it with great success a quarter of a century later. Rarely, if ever, did he fail to read the notes correctly, but he was forever coming in ahead of time, with the result that he created more harsh discords than any other man of his generation.

And in this connection a disturbing thought intrudes. Just before he died, down in Tennessee, Bryan startled the world by playing a rather hideous fantasia on the theme of government suppres-

[53]

sion of free opinion. Was he even then merely anticipating? God forbid! And yet ten years afterward Harvard University crawled before the Massachusetts legislature, children were expelled from Philadelphia schools, and refused diplomas in New York schools for refusing to salute the flag, the shadow of Fascism seemed to stretch athwart the land. One dare not assert very confidently that Bryan was less than a prophet, even at Dayton.

Men say that both Clay and Bryan were thrown off, at least to some extent, by that most imperishable of human aspirations, the hope of being President. It may be. At any rate, the amateur player understands only too well how easy it is to slip by trying to read ahead. But the amateur player, by the same token, is likely to judge them somewhat leniently in consideration of the fact that they never enjoyed the advantage of being cued in. Whether it is by the baton of Stokowski, by Charity flourishing a ruler, or by the iron hand of Fate, not a few great successes are due in part to being thrust in the right direction at the right moment. Consider Theodore Roosevelt, who was cued in by the crack of Czolgosz's pistol; it is not in derogation of the brilliance of his subsequent performance to note that he was literally compelled to come in at the right time.

And what strength of character it takes to be cued in wrong and still remain unruffled! Indeed, not a few of the Christian virtues, as well as the worldly arts, are exercised and strengthened by this process. At rehearsal you find between the letters E and F nothing but a thick bar with the figure "11" over it; eleven measures' rest, which is well, for beginning at F is a neat little solo, where you can shine, if you can just get the count right. And for once you get it, for Charity's down beat has the emphasis of a circus canvasman driving tent pegs; at eight you place your fingers, at nine you flex your arms, at ten you draw a long breath, just after eleven you lift the embouchure to your lips—and Charity says, "Rotten! Go back to E and try it again." Oh, well—life is like that. At any rate, your count was right, and if you have done it once you can do it again. They're off, and you have it; yes, there's that little staccato passage the first violin has in the sixth; there's the 'cello coming in on the ninth; your count is absolutely right, *ten*-two-three-four, *eleven*-two-three-fo——"For Heaven's sake!" says Charity, "have the third violins left the room altogether? Go back to E and get some volume into it." Alas! for a lost

solo! And it would have been a swell one, too.
You feel it in your bones that you would have
played it just right. But never mind. After all, you
have had plenty of time to get your breath, the
rhythm is firmly fixed in your head now, you remember the little curlicue with which the first
violin finishes the eleventh measure, and you
know exactly how much of a split second afterward you must strike in. You are all set to go and
as the rest come howling down to the point—
plenty of volume this time—for once you don't
feel as if you were standing in the middle of a
race-track, under the wire, while ten horses come
thundering down the stretch, neck and neck.
Steady, certain, rejoicing in your own assurance,
you whip the flute to your lips—and Charity claps
her hand dramatically to her forehead, exclaiming:
"Ragged, ragged beyond belief! Go back to E
and do it over!"

Patience on a monument is a poor simile indeed
for the flute-player just bursting to play a solo
and not allowed to get to it! Such a man, after a
little practice of this kind, should be able to listen
to an account of anybody's operation without the
least difficulty; he should be able to discuss economics with a single-taxer, or reassemble the con-
tents of an upset card-index file, or read the state

papers of Herbert Hoover without nervous exhaustion; for, as regards the great virtue of patience, he has been tried as by fire.

All the same, this art of coming in is, at best, but a utilitarian art, to be cultivated only for its effects, not for itself. Hence anything that tends to simplify it has my warm approval. I am charmed, for example, by information received from a correspondent in Iowa. Out where the tall corn grows they believe in getting things done by the easiest and least complicated method—or they did twenty years ago when my correspondent was a member of an Iowan ensemble much like ours. The resourceful leader of this group came upon a complicated repeat sign, printed *D. C. al* ⌒; but did he gum the works by any such incomprehensible command as *"Da Capo al fermata"*? Not he; he shouted, "Dee See to the hog's eye!" and the thing was done. If you choose to make a test case of it, probably this expedient was entirely unconstitutional; but it got 'em back, which, after all, was the point.

In music, as in life, it is necessary to cultivate the art of coming in, and I, for one, am ready to lift my hat admiringly to the man who masters it, for it is the strong foundation on which success, in life as in music, is built. Nevertheless, I propose to cherish, inwardly, a mental reservation. I hope to maintain, unexpressed and imperceptible, just a slight touch of disdain toward such people; for I have encountered, in life and in music, certain individuals who can come in with the greatest accuracy and precision, but who, having come in, play so harshly and so much out of tune, or so thinly and sourly, that their room is preferable to their company. Not infrequently they collect garlands and salvos of applause, fortune, and fame among the unthinking. All the same, there are plenty of glittering successes who are withal so empty that the judicious infinitely prefer the company of elephantine blunderers, men too heavy or too furious to keep exactly to the beat, but who, when they do crash through, bear down everything that stands in their way. There are failures in the world more magnificent than nine out of ten successes.

At any rate, this is a fine philosophy for one who will never come in right, anyway.

A Moral Equivalent for Athletics

A MORAL EQUIVALENT FOR
ATHLETICS

A CELEBRATED conductor, foreign born but long resident in this country, recently asserted that the trouble with music in America is that

"People stay home from concerts to play quartets in the wrong key, with the wrong notes, in the wrong tempo, and think they are doing so much for the future of music."

This man has fairly earned a position in music which makes anything he says in that field important; unfortunately, this reputation will cause many people to take him seriously when he ventures out of the field of music and into that of philosophy, as he did in this quotation. And that, as the North Carolina farmer said from the tree top where the freshet had deposited him to his children who were lamenting his demise with shrill screams below, "That is how all these damn lies git about the country."

For the highly skilled and highly trained professional musician is, of all men, the man least likely to know why amateurs play quartets, or why

amateurs play anything. There are a few exceptions, of course. Mr. Sigmund Spaeth, for instance,
seems to know, and so do Mr. Robert Haven
Schauffler, Mrs. Catharine Drinker Bowen, and a
few others. These intelligentsia, however, can
probably be counted on the fingers, and I do not
think there is a foreigner among them. This is no
cause for astonishment, since the problem is not a
matter of understanding music, but of understanding Americans. Indeed, it should not be expected
of alien musicians among us. If they understand
their art, that is enough; when they cause pertur-
bation by misinterpreting the national character,
the fault is ours for expecting them to be psychol-
ogists, as well as musicians.

The distinguished musician quoted above may,
therefore, be forgiven for his utterance, since he
could not reasonably be expected to know what
he was talking about. What is unpardonable is
that his remark was widely quoted in this country
with respect, if not always with approval. Apparently there are native sons so dull of understanding that they actually believe that the amateur
quartet player is the national stayer-away from
concerts. Yet no mental, but only a visual, process
is needed to dissipate that illusion; let the observer
attend a concert and look about him. He need not

think; he need do no more than look, because the amateurs will be there.

It may be objected that even a foreign-born conductor ought to be capable of that, hence he has no more excuse to err than the native. But the cases are not the same. The foreigner may look as hard as he can, but he will not see the audience, he will see the empty seats; and he cannot disabuse his mind of the error that those who are not in them are at home playing quartets. Only an American can understand that those Americans who stay away from concerts would regard the idea of playing quartets with the same horror and shame that would fill the soul of a European at the idea of carrying a package on the street for his wife. The reactions are identical because they are aroused by the same stimuli; neither the American asked to play nor the European asked to carry a package really objects to the trifling physical labor involved; it is the social stigma the act would put upon him that he cannot endure.

Perhaps the American born and bred in one of the largest dozen cities of the country may find this hard to believe; but one brought up in the country, or in a small American town, will understand at once. To this day, in large sections of the country, music is a slightly shameful mystery, as far as men are concerned. Sinclair Lewis satirized this attitude brilliantly in one of the most tragic pages of that supremely tragic history, *Babbitt*. When the proposal was made that the Rotary Club support the project to establish a symphony orchestra in Zenith, the members really wanted to do it, but each, before casting his vote in favor of the project, felt that his own self-respect demanded that he clear himself of any suspicion of liking symphonic music; they justified voting for the orchestra by assuring themselves that it would be a fine advertisement for Zenith. The vice of music, they agreed, would be counteracted by the virtue of advertising.

The general assumption has been that this proves one thing, and one thing only, to wit, that Babbitt is a fool. That this is true is hardly open to doubt, but that it is the whole truth is by no means so certain. The fact that the European objects violently to carrying a package on the street likewise proves that he is a fool, but it also implies the existence of a long series of social concepts and attitudes, which accounts for the existence of the folly and its prevalence over wide areas. Is it not reasonable to suppose that behind Mr. Babbitt's objection to confessing a liking for symphonic music—and for chamber music, opera and the recitals of most virtuosi, as well—there may be a similar complication of forces?

Note that the conventions of Zenith do not impose a stigma on appreciation of all forms of music, but only on serious music. Toward the end of the late depression I heard Paul Whiteman, in a lecture at a famous conservatory, pose a question that has not been answered. He stated that every week he had to meet a huge payroll; I am afraid to quote from memory, but the figure was far up in the thousands. He said that there were in this country at least five organizations similar to his which met comparable payrolls; he was inclined to think some of them were even larger than his. These payrolls had been met regularly, right through the depression, and met with money which Mr. Babbitt cheerfully paid as admission fees. At the moment when Mr. Whiteman spoke, the Metropolitan Opera was making frantic appeals for financial support to avoid closing its doors. Practically every big symphony orchestra in the country was also cadging for funds, and the very conservatory in which he spoke was financially distressed. Why, asked Mr. Whiteman, can jazz not only pay its way, but return a handsome profit to its practitioners, while the music which most of the world has agreed is the finest is dependent upon alms?

Part of the answer unquestionably lies in the fact that Mr. Babbitt can afford to boast of having attended a concert by Paul Whiteman, but feels it necessary to make an elaborate explanation of why he attended a concert by Fritz Kreisler. I venture to doubt that this is altogether to Mr. Babbitt's discredit. He knows that nobody goes to a Whiteman concert unless he wants to hear the music; and he also knows that, in the smaller cities and towns, a great many people attend classical concerts, not because they want to hear the music, but because they wish to make the neighbors think they like to hear classical music. He detests that form of hypocrisy and snobbery. Unfortunately, his recoil from it throws him straight into the opposite hypocrisy of pretending to dislike classical music when, sometimes, in his heart he likes it. All the same, the initial recoil from sham is not discreditable.

There is, however, an American—and his tribe increases—who has escaped that inhibition. He is the one who plays quartets at home—in the wrong key, perhaps, with the wrong notes and in the wrong tempo—but who doesn't do it for the future of music, but for pure sport. He need not neces-

sarily be musical at all, within any reasonable def-
inition of the term; all he must have is an ear not
completely tone-deaf, and a high appreciation of
ingenuity and dexterity. With this equipment only
he cannot hope ever to produce music worth pre-
senting to an audience, but he may very easily develop into a downright rabid concert-goer; and
if we develop some millions of rabid concert-
goers, the future, if not of music, at least of professional musicians in this country, is assured.

I am not guessing about this. I know it beyond
peradventure, because I happen to be a recondi-
tioned Babbit myself. The inscrutable dispensa-
tions of providence gave me a youth spent in
typical American villages and small cities, with
an ear so dull that I can no more tune a fiddle than
I can whip Joe Louis. The fire of genius that
burned in the young Mozart, if it ever touched
me, encountered an asbestos soul which emerged
not even slightly charred. I had, moreover, observed the sort of people who professed to go into
ecstasies over every wandering concertizer who
drifted our way, and I knew that a large percent-
age of them were frauds of the first order. Music?
Bah! Oh, a barber-shop quartette was all right,
and a brass band was usually made up of honest
workmen who were entitled to as much respect

as competent brick masons; but violinists and singers of art songs were fishermen for suckers. Honest men evaded their nets.

Furthermore, to this day I remain only slightly more musical than a wooden cigar Indian; yet nowadays I go to concerts and have a grand time, although I still have some slight difficulty in distinguishing between "La Paloma" and the "Habañera" from *Carmen*; and even the Strauss waltzes consist of two, the other being the one that isn't "The Blue Danube." Understand music? God save the mark! What I have at last discovered is that this great realm is not exclusively the province of those whose ears are keenly attuned to the beauty of sound and whose emotional response is swift and unerring. There is also room in it for those whose talents and aspirations run no higher than to the satisfaction of the sporting instinct.

This discovery I owe to the process branded as the ruin of American music—the process of playing terribly as a member of a terrible ensemble at home. If our group has any virtue at all, it isn't a musician's, but a sportsman's virtue, to wit, a genuine admiration of form for its own sake and not for the sake of the gallery. This is not necessarily allied with skill. The poor dub who slams everything into the net may yet cherish a keen admiration, and even a theoretical understanding of the miracles of skill and balance that the great Tilden used to perform on the tennis-court. Certainly he appreciates and understands them better than a man who never held a racket in his hands; and if he plays his best, he is a tennis-player, all right.

Our ensemble, I think, has consistently played its best. At any rate, it has avoided gallery play, for no audiences are permitted. In my youth I should have asked, if you play for nobody, then why play at all? And I should have been astonished if anyone had countered with the question, do you play duck pins for the bystanders, or stud poker for the kibitzers? Yet the question is a fair one. If you are up to professional form, play for an audience, by all means; but that isn't the only reason for playing. There remains the game for the game's sake. I am convinced that the musical sterility of America, about which we are always hearing, is due in no small part to the fact that it has occurred to so few Americans that it is possible to play the "Jupiter" symphony for the same reasons that one plays duck pins, or stud, and to derive the same sort of satisfactions from it.

Consider, if you please, wherein lies the fascination of these two games. There is an element of chance in both, but in bowling everything depends on the player's own body; no great strength is required, but coördination, timing, balance are supremely important. At cards, on the other hand, much depends upon the other players, or rather on one's own speed and accuracy in calculating what the other players are going to do. Rest assured that both these elements are of vital importance in playing in an amateur ensemble. The moment of greatest tenseness in bowling is the instant after the ball has left your hand and started down the alley; before it has traveled ten feet you know whether it is rightly or wrongly placed, and, if it is right, to watch it describe its long, flat trajectory with a hook at the end that brings it crashing into the apex of the triangle of pins— well, if you have ever bowled, you know what it is.

Now the "Jupiter" is notable for the relatively even use it makes of all the instruments. No matter what you are playing, you will find a dozen places in your part where you are called on for a long, sustained note, followed by a staccato run of very short ones that is supposed to wind up with a bang squarely on the tonic or the dominant. I suppose that to a skillful musician this means nothing much; but a rank amateur finds that the success of this operation depends largely on the start. If that first note is well struck, the effect is very much like launching a bowling-ball properly. Thereafter the thing pretty well takes care of itself; you shoot down the alley—I should say the staff—spinning in a beautiful curve, and at the end crash into the midst of the other instruments, scattering bright harmonies in every direction as the pins are hurled wildly by a strike. But, oh, if you don't hit the first one right! Down you go, scrambling madly to recover the pitch, but edging, edging, edging off to right or left, sharp or flat, finally to hit the gutter with a thud conventionally, but correctly, described as dull and sickening. From the very first instant you know that it is all wrong, but if you are a genuine amateur, one of the really hopeless kind, there is nothing under God's heaven you can do about it.

This is, however, only half of it. In bowling you act alone; but in this game there is a whole roomful of other amateurs participating. Most poker-players, probably superstitiously, like to sit, as they say, "under the gun," that is, next to the dealer. In an amateur ensemble there is no superstition about it. To be placed right at the conductor is a distinct, solid, substantial advantage, for no amateur ever knew his music any too well, and it is a grave risk to lift one's eyes from the page even to catch the beat. Near the leader, however, you can sense it, even if you don't actually see it, and this tends to lift self-confidence to the level of arrogance. The amateur under the gun can bear down, override, and trample all opposition, and he usually does so. But when you are sitting back a little, then comes the psychological test. The deal has started and let us suppose you are playing the "Jupiter." The moment is approaching when you must pick up the theme. Now it is not only a matter of playing it correctly yourself, but also of figuring what that clarinet player at your elbow has in the hole. By all that is right and proper it should be nothing but a low, smooth, sustaining tone to heighten, by contrast, the brightness of yours. But since he is an amateur, this is a game of chance, and he is as likely as not to turn up a joker in the shape of a reedy squawk that Israfel, whose heart-strings are a lute, could not cover harmoniously.

Horrified musicians perhaps will be shocked to the soul by the idea of making a game of one of the world's masterpieces. That is one of the things that are the matter with music. It is too full of horrified musicians, too easily horrified by every contact of music with common humanity. They have pretty well succeeded in withdrawing it from contact with American humanity, with the result that Paul Whiteman's jazz band flourishes prodigiously, while the Metropolitan Opera goes begging. The jazz-players, at any rate, must be credited with remembering the pit whence they were digged. Any art that becomes altogether arty and in no wise common, is a dead art and should be disposed of like any other cadaver.

Fortunately, however, the world still possesses musicians who are not horrified, who, indeed, are practically unhorrifiable. The amateur who is in it for sport and who encounters one of these is in luck. I remember a white night some fifteen years ago when I sat in a Greek restaurant—the only place open at midnight—in a small Southern town with Efrem Zimbalist and heard him, over a steak and potatoes, telling a young violinist whom he had encountered by chance, how to play Bach's "Air for the G string." Everything connected with the fiddle is Greek to me, and I remember nothing that he said, but I do remember my stupefaction at discovering in a man whom everybody called a great artist simplicity, kindliness, deep understanding of plain men, and sudden outbursts of sly humor. I was even more ignorant then than I am now; it did not cross my mind that it would have been much more remarkable to discover a really first-rate man who doesn't possess some of these qualities.

Wolfgang Amadeus Mozart was a first-rate man. I do not believe for a moment that he would be horrified at the mauling our ensemble gives his "Jupiter" symphony—that is, as long as the mauling is due to the fact that we can't play it, and not to any disposition intentionally to add to it innovations of our own. There is a tremendous difference between sand-lot baseball that is nothing else, and an exhibition game for the spectators. For the amateur who tackles before an audience music that he can't play, I have no defense; he deserves the withering comments that musicians make on his performance. But he is not the subject of this discussion; we are considering "people who stay home to play." On these there is only one limitation—the music must be music that they like, or the business will become a bore.

Any man who likes to bowl, or to draw to a three-card flush, would like to play the "Jupiter" if he suspected half of what is in it. But he will soon discover that this is no game for short sports; taking down the two corner pins for a spare or filling an inside straight is child's play by comparison with fitting together the parts of the fugal section of the last movement. Obviously, it can be done, for the thing is played by the great orchestras constantly; but the amateur whose proudest achievement has been to carry the air of "Drink to Me Only with Thine Eyes" isn't going to do it. More than that, and worse than that, he isn't going to know why, for the notes are easy, and unless his conductor is trying to imitate Beecham, the time is not confusing. So the amateur will wax wroth and, like a pressing golfer, make a worse mess of it than ever; after which, if he is a prudent man, he will calm down and begin to consider the lie of the land. And then, perhaps, he will begin to get an inkling of a curious fact, to wit, that this Mozart, as I have heard it put, is one of the easiest composers to perform, and one of the hardest to play that ever lived. This is, perhaps, the beginning of a musical education; but it is certainly the beginning of a resolution that the next time the "Jupiter" is on the program of a competent orchestra, you will be there, paying particular attention to this section just to see how the infernal thing is supposed to go.

There you are. There is the complete answer to the complaint of the musician quoted at the beginning of this article. The people who at home play quartets, or symphonies, in the wrong key, with the wrong notes, in the wrong tempo, don't stay away from concerts. They can't afford to. Their reasons may be all wrong. Their motives may be low. Their attitudes may be reprehensible. But they attend, and their money swells the box-office receipts just as effectively as that of the righteous.

More than that, they get their money's worth. I do not assume to say that they get what the truly musical get. Probably they do not. There are people to whom music is meat and drink, the very staff of life, and what they experience at a great concert must be far beyond the comprehension of those of us who are not dowered with that gift of God, high appreciation of music.

But quite ordinary fellows, as I know by experience, get their money's worth. It is, in the beginning, the delight of the sand-lot baseball-player in the Polo Grounds, the dub tennis-player at Forest Hills, the gallery of heavy handicaps watching Gene Sarazen tee up. Here on the podium is a champion, with a hundred-odd big leaguers in the semicircle before him. Here are form, speed, power, precision, all in ample measure. Here, at last, the thing is going to be done right, every shot placed to a hair's-breadth, every backhand drive like artillery fire, every smash timed to a split second. Now we shall see exactly where our ensemble has been so consistently muffing it, and if we are no more able to do it ourselves, nevertheless we shall rejoice in having seen the thing put over.

So they come to the last movement and the fugue begins to build up. Perhaps we have heard the "Jupiter" before, but in the wild welter of sound who could pick out those slight, tentative beginnings, if he had not seen them on paper, had not gone over them a dozen times, never getting them quite right? But having done that, who could miss them, now that the conductor is lifting them, apparently picking them out with the tip of his baton, from the rich embroidery of the symphony? Now the violins take it and a measure later the 'cellos ought to come in; they do, but how is this? This is not the music our ensemble plays, this roar from the deep, this chorus of singing Titans. It is the fugue, all right, but what, oh, Lord! has happened to it? Here, where the thin piping of our flutes supplied the third voice, comes a shout from the wood-wind choir, strong, clear, airy, and yet piercing, caught instantly, borne along and whirled away by the triumphant strings.

Well played, magnificently played, but—after all, what was it? Perfect timing, perfect balance, perfect coördination, yes, these we can understand

and appreciate; have we not been striving for these very things for weeks? These are what we came for, what we paid our money for. These constitute Symphony No. 41, in C major. But out of them has risen something more, something unaccountable and confusing, something arising out of the music, but not the music—at least not the game we have been playing, but something which we might have passed unperceived had we not played the game. The game, played as it should be played, is transformed into something else; so one begins to perceive, dimly, why this thing, already sufficiently named, is also called by the name of the king of the gods.

Here, though, we begin to trespass on forbidden ground. These matters are for true musicians, not for amateurs who practice mayhem on good music for their own amusement. All the same, we return to our ensemble more determined than ever. The game is a good game; never mind the art. Spread Mozart's pages on your music-racks and prepare for crime. Let us play.

The Necessary Dash of Bitters

THE NECESSARY DASH OF BITTERS

CHARITY laid down her ruler and surrendered. This was highly significant, for Charity is ordinarily an indomitable individual. But there is a limit to the endurance even of an iron woman, and Charity reached it at last.

The occasion was an assault upon the Mozart quartet in D major for flute and strings, and the proximate cause of Charity's collapse, defeat, and complete rout was the total inability of the flute to make the grade. This was ruinous because, as the name implies, if the flute is out of this particular work, what you have left is emptier than the Democratic party without Roosevelt. No true amateur ensemble expects ever to carry through an attack on any important piece of music without suffering casualties, but in general the outfit can contrive to limp along even if one member after another is shot from under it. If, however, what you are playing is a quartet for flute and strings and the flute drops dead, well, now, I ask you, could even Charity, the indomitable, be expected to hold out? I couldn't blame her, and if I couldn't, who could? I was playing the flute.

A Little Night-Music

The point of this sad story, the thing that gives it substance and significance, is the fact that I know that music. I pretend to no ability whatever as a sight reader. Set before me a sheet of music that I never saw before, and I disclaim any responsibility for what transpires thereafter. As a blatant amateur I am not a whit abashed by this; but when the music on the rack is the D major quartet, which I have gone over time and again, which I know measure by measure, and note by note, and which is not particularly difficult to begin with, then inability to play it is more than merely failure to rise to the level of professional standards of musicianship. It raises doubts not of musical, but of mental, competence. It brings one up with a bang squarely against the basic futility of human existence.

It is distressing. It is depressing. It is mortifying in the extreme. It is filled with the bitterness of unrequited love and quinine. Yet suspicion lingers that in some obscure fashion it may be tonic also, and that it is, in fact, one of the elements of value to amateurs in playing music. Certainly there are few things better designed to humble intellectual arrogance and induce humility. To translate into practice what one knows in theory is hard, very hard; yet in our inane way we are apt to plume ourselves on a lot of theoretical knowledge that really doesn't mean a thing. Frequently we get away with it, too. I know that in newspaper work, and I suspect that in psychiatry, dentistry and the real estate business as well, a man is not always compelled to call his shots in advance; and if he pockets the wrong ball, he can mask his surprise with a smirk and shove up another counter on his score. This is demoralizing; this ought not to happen, but it does.

It doesn't happen in ensemble-playing, however. There your shots are called for you—set down in black and white, on the conductor's score as well as on your own, and usually unmistakably indicated, if not actually printed, on the other parts as well. If the composer has written an ascending chromatic scale ending in E flat, it is E flat you must pocket and not any other note whatsoever. More than that, it must be a straight shot across the board, too. It will not do to carom off three cushions and the eight-ball, first, even if you end by triumphantly knocking the E flat into the pocket; because in your wild career you will have disrupted the entire ensemble and all the other players will be thirsting for your blood.

Doubtless one measure of the difference between an artisan and an artist is the fact that if the former does his job even moderately well the gap between his original concept and his final product is so small as to be negligible; whereas the practitioner of a great art must do extremely well or the gap between his concept and his product will be appalling. Choice of a low standard is of great assistance in inflating one's vanity. Indeed, I myself can start with the concept of "Listen to the Mocking Bird," and if the end product isn't exactly "Listen to the Mocking Bird," it approximates it so closely that it couldn't very well be mistaken for anything else; whereas when I start with the concept of the flute part of the D-major quartet, the end product is such that Charity, the iron woman, lays down her ruler and, wailing, quits.

Does this not discourage me? Of course it does. But the discouragement, not being vital, is not paralyzing. I do not depend upon music for a living, so my inability to play doesn't induce suicidal tendencies. A bit of discouragement, now and then, in non-vital matters is probably not bad for any of us. It tends to reduce the Napoleonic delusion; as has been said of humor, it fulfills the function of the slave who followed Cæsar to remind him in the midst of his triumph that he was bald.

A professional musician who could not play the

notes on a sheet of music before him I suppose would be in the position of a newspaper reporter who could not hit any of the right keys on his typewriter; he ought, first, to try sleeping it off, and if that didn't work, he ought to have an inquiring neurologist rap on his knee-caps. But an amateur who cannot play is, contrary to the opinion of the neighbors, not under any obligation to go hang himself immediately. This assertion of his freedom presupposes, of course, that he has not deliberately invited the neighbors in to hear him; if he has done that, then the situation is reversed and the obligation is plain.

Yet there are violent men who, confronted with this baffling situation, have flung aside their instruments and quit cold. All that one can say of such cases is that it is really just too bad; for the persons who quit in disgust obviously are just the ones who ought to stick it out. The very violence of their reaction to a touch of bitterness is evidence that they need it—very much as the man whose arm gets sorest is he who most needed to be vaccinated.

I am talking, of course, about the ineluctable failures. If a man can't play because he hasn't practiced, that is another matter. If he picks up a wind instrument and attempts to play it with a fever blister on his lip, or one of the strings and tries to play it with a sprained finger; or if the light is dim, or the edition is badly printed; if some one has opened a window behind him and a cascade of air right out of Siberia is pouring down his neck; if the man at his elbow blandly refuses to admit that there is any such thing as an accidental, or the fellow opposite insists on beating time with a foot encased in a freshly shined shoe that sparkles and glitters like the mouth of hell itself; if the first violin starts a quarter-tone off pitch and eases further away with each successive measure, or if the pianist exhibits about as much sense of rhythm as a cook-stove falling downstairs—in any or all of these cases there is cause for indignation, but not for bitterness. These are but normal incidents of life in an amateur ensemble, which sensible men accept as philosophically as they do blizzards, politicians, insurance agents, and dinner hosts who ice the claret. Wrath is an entirely different emotion from despair.

The failure under consideration here is the failure without excuse. It stalks behind everyone who undertakes to play music or who tries to practice any other great art. With the amateur musician it is usually a failure in technique, but even the master of technique doesn't escape it. I cannot play the Mozart quartet, because, while I know the music, my lip is leathery and my fingers are slow and clumsy. However, the best violinist of my acquaintance, a man to whom all the tricks of technique long ago became second nature, a man who can perform at sight any music ever written by any great composer, tells me that in twenty years of assiduous practice he has played just one phrase of Mozart exactly as he thinks the master intended it to be played. He performs Mozart's music constantly and admirably; his performances have brought him applause and a lordly reputation in the musical world; and he is not ill-content, because technical dexterity carries a man far in the world. He cannot justly be denied the title of virtuoso now, but he will call himself master-artist on the day when he plays not a phrase, but an entire page as he thinks Mozart imagined it. However, he frankly admits that he supposes when that happens the conductor will be the angel Israfel and his instrument, not a violin, but a harp.

I am no artist of any sort and very far from being a musical artist. As long as I live, I shall be engrossed primarily with the problem of sounding the note at all. If I live longer than Händel, or Haydn, or even Leopold Auer, I shall never arrive

at the point at which technique is a question of
minor importance and interpretation everything.
But one need not be an artist to know the taste of
frustration. Right at the beginning of this same
D major quartet there is a measure consisting of
a little run of sixteenth notes—perfectly simple,
perfectly plain, such a trifle as anyone having had
a couple of lessons on the flute ought to be able
to play, merely a small ripple on the surface of the
melody. And I can run through it, sounding every
note and ending the measure in time; but when I
do so, it isn't a rippling passage, it is a wabbling
passage, and the difference is all the difference between Lazarus in Abraham's bosom and Dives
being in torment.

Then why not chuck it? Why continue to struggle with difficulties that I shall never overcome,
or which, if I did overcome them, would by their
removal merely unmask other and more formidable difficulties, and so on, world without end?
Why turn for recreation to any art, knowing in
advance that all art is tinged with the bitterness
of frustration?

Well, why drop tincture of gentian into a cock-
tail? It has a villainous taste straight, and sophisticated with angostura bark, quassia, and the like
it tastes even worse. Yet what people would think

of a man who served old-fashioneds without any bitters is beyond expression. Properly mingled with suaver ingredients, its villainy becomes merely an accent, underscoring their various excellencies, compounding their antagonisms, strengthening their affinities, and introducing into their relations a genial warmth that rescues the whole from flatness and monotony.

I submit that a man, and especially an American, who makes his living doing something that he can do fairly well may improve the taste of life appreciably by choosing for his hobby something too difficult for him ever to do expertly. This rules out most forms of sport, for a man who can make a true hobby of any form of sport is pretty much of an adolescent. It rules out the lower forms of mechanics. Carpentry, for example, is not a good hobby, because a man clever with his hands can soon carry carpentry as far as any reasonable human being cares to go. Lift it a notch or two, though, into the realm of cabinet-making and you have entered the field of art. It is improbable in the extreme that the best amateur cabinet-maker is ever going to rival Duncan Phyfe, not to mention Sheraton or Heppelwhite. Up to the day when the amateur is too old and feeble to lift a tool there will still be a curve that needs more grace, still a

finish lacking the velvety softness that his imagination has created but that his hands haven't.

Assume that your amateur cabinet-maker is in
his true vocation an eminently successful man.
Suppose he is, for example, a bond salesman so
great that he could go out tomorrow and sell
bonds of the Confederate States of America to
Andrew Mellon at par. Suppose that his life is
otherwise so placid and satisfactory that he has
never seen the inside of a jail, a divorce court, or a
Senate investigating committee room. Suppose, in
short, that his draught in the chalice of life is
mixed with none but sound, mellow, aged-in-the-
wood ingredients. Nevertheless, the dash of bitterness injected into it whenever he looks at the
table that he just can't get quite right brings out
the flavor of all the rest and vastly improves the
whole.

Taking us by and large, we Americans are a
pretty successful lot. I say that without for a
moment forgetting the millions of exceptions. I
remember clearly the existence of such people as
the unemployed, the Baltimore lady who isn't a
queen, and Mr. Landon. Nevertheless, I stick to
it that the proportion in the total population of
people who have achieved at least moderate suc-

cess is larger in the United States than in any other country in the world.

But to draw the obvious inference that we are therefore the happiest people in the world is a little more than I am prepared to do. Easy living is no guarantee of happiness, as every psychiatric and neurological clinic in the country can demonstrate. Suicides among us are not by any means confined to the unemployed and the poverty-stricken. There is little convincing evidence that Americans, even the more successful, are conspicuously well equipped to enjoy the world, no matter how far they have chased the wolf from the door.

On the contrary, there is an impressive body of evidence to support the theory that American life, despite the soundness and agreeable flavor of its ingredients, is a little flat on the tongues of some of our most successful citizens after they have passed, say, fifty. There are far more Americans than men of any other nation who, at fifty, have accumulated enough to keep them and their wives in great comfort, and even in modest luxury, for the rest of their lives; but there are very few Americans who retire from business, or from professional practice, while they are still mentally and physically vigorous. When one does withdraw, he does so at the price of a sharp reduction in prestige, not infrequently involving suspicion that his intellectual faculties are tottering, if not collapsing. Americans, say the neighbors, scornfully, are not quitters; from street-sweeper right up to Supreme Court justice, they stay in the ring until they are knocked cold, or until Death strikes the gong and the round is over.

If this were incontrovertible evidence that we are a stout-hearted race, it might well be a matter of national pride. Unfortunately, though, there is another explanation that will account for the facts just as well. This explanation is that we don't quit for the simple, but not altogether flattering, reason that we can't quit. We are like highly specialized organs of the body; we must continue functioning in one specialized way because we have lost the power, if we ever had it, to function in any other way.

If he retires from business at fifty, what can the ordinary American do but die? What else does he do? Certainly, if he takes up in a really big way any debauchery involving wine and women, he will pass out of the picture with great speed. If he harbors the illusion that because his head is clear, his eye alert, his stomach still competent, and his blood pressure somewhere within reason, therefore he has the physical endurance he had at twenty-five and decides to devote his time to developing a really good game of tennis, he is a gone coon. Even if he confines himself to as decorous and aldermanly a game as golf, thirty-six holes a day will probably put him under the sod pretty soon. Besides, how can a man who has been accustomed for many years to wrestling with real problems, which only a full-grown man can hope to handle, get any kick out of sports at which a nineteen-year-old sophomore, with never a brain cell working, can give him a fearful trimming and not even extend himself?

Countless Americans hug the delusion that for the proper enjoyment of life a man needs only money and leisure, plus fairly good health. It is a cruel misconception. For sports he needs youth, as well as money and leisure; and for anything else he needs preparation running back through many years—come to think of it, he needs youth there, too, for he needs something that began when he was fairly young.

For a case in point, take travel. A man with money and leisure, and nothing else, cannot travel; he can only go. He may cause his body to be transported over thousands of miles; he may acquire an aching head and an awful case of museum feet; he may become familiar with all the time-tables of all the continents; and he may develop a burning personal hatred of every hotel-keeper between Liverpool and Shanghai, both inclusive, with no resources other than money and leisure. But this is merely going, not traveling. Really to travel, a man must take along with him a sufficient fund, not of money only, but of appreciation of the significance of what he is going to see; and this fund cannot be accumulated in a day, or a week, or a month, or a year.

Nor is it likely to be acquired by constant attendance at the public library and faithful perusal of the books there. This will give a man information, but not experience except as, by a feat of imagination, he may be able to gain experience at second hand. This is at best but a carbon copy of the original; but the man who has made a mess of any art is in far better position to appreciate the work of men who have made a success of any art. A man who has tried to play Mozart, and failed, through that vain effort comes into position better to understand the man who tried to paint the Sistine Madonna, and did. The defeated musician at least knows how it feels to be up against the impossible that is made impossible by the feebleness of one's own resources. Thus he begins to get some conception, even though a dim one, of the truth that the greatest artistic masterpiece represents only the failure of a nobler plan, that Raphael imagined something greater than the Sistine Madonna, Ictinus than the Parthenon, Michelangelo than the David. Thus the mightiest works of the human hand become to him merely suggestive of the greater achievements of the human spirit, conceptions so great that no hand could execute them.

I am by no means certain that this will make him a better man, but it will assuredly make him no worse; and it will assist marvelously in entertaining him in the years when younger men are pushing him out of business, when the doctors are taking away his cigars and cocktails, and when advancing age is making him a model of propriety. Surely there is no figure more truly pitiable than the man of high intelligence who has devoted that intelligence, exclusive of all else, to something that is bound to lose its flavor just about the time he reaches full maturity, and who finds at the very moment when he is prepared to enjoy the fruits of his long labor that he has mixed himself a draught that, however excellent, is flat and tasteless.

Moralists never tire of denouncing us as a pleasure-mad people. Perhaps they are right, but hardly in the sense which they attach to the phrase. It is not our avidity for pleasure that is the sad thing, but the fact that so many of our pleasures are no fun; and to chase furiously after pleasure in which there is no fun is indubitably a crazy procedure. But the saddest, and the maddest, of our diversions is not the chase frankly after pleasure, but the chase after "cultural values" that are no fun, either. I suppose the immense widening of experience that attends contact, as a hard-working student, with one of the arts, is a cultural value, but I hate to admit it, because that links it up with lecture courses, and discussion groups, and selected reading lists, and all the fol-de-rol that has gone far toward establishing the American belief that a cultured man is one who is able, when any subject whatsoever is introduced, to say nothing about it in not less than five hundred words.

It is not that the American search after culture is ineffective; on the contrary, it produces some of the most formidable people imaginable. I remember the sprightly lady to whom the idiot who presented me gave what she considered a cue with the word "music." Instantly she was off. "Oh, I am simply wild about modern Spanish music," she declared, in the manner of Norfolk, earl marshal, proclaiming a new king. Well, as we used to say in the South, she had me in a split stick. I don't know anything about Spanish music, but something had to be said, so after a moment's desperate mental scrambling I murmured a word or two about De Falla, hoping faintly that I **had pro-**nounced it right. "What?" she asked, so I knew I hadn't, but tried again. "I don't believe I know that," she returned, thoughtfully, "but I am crazy about the rhumba and the tango." A thrice-blessed manservant arrived at that moment with a tray, and Blücher was no more welcome to Welington at Waterloo. I never got the lady's name, but I remember her as the Shulamite, for to me she is terrible as an army with banners.

The man who devotes himself to alcohol, or amour, or the development of the striated muscles with such assiduity as to land himself in the graveyard or the lunatic asylum is assuredly a fool; but I am inclined to think that he is as Socrates is to Simple Simon by comparison with the man who fritters away his life seeking "cultural values" that do not amuse him. The frankly non-intellectual fool does have a good time for a short while; the solemn ass may live longer, but why should he want to?

I speak with vibrant emotion upon this subject, for I have been just such a one myself. When I was younger and, as I choose to believe, sillier than I am now, I put in enormous quantities of time trying to understand music by listening to it. Doubtless this would have worked had I been musical to begin with; Henry Adams says it worked in his case and I have no reason to doubt that it did. But I happen to be one of those individuals to whom harmony is a closed book, and an appreciation of melody alone doesn't carry you far when you are listening to a hundred and twenty-five instruments playing a Brahms symphony, not to mention one of the productions of Prokofiev, Hindemith or Honneger. It was a melancholy endeavor, this search of the blind man in a dark room for the black cat that wasn't there; but I pursued it with an assiduity worthy of a more hopeful cause, and after every evening in a concert-hall, straining my ears to take in an incomprehensible uproar, I went away as stuffed with the consciousness of virtue as an Indian fakir arising from his bed of spikes.

Some surviving shreds of common sense prevented me from adopting any such attitude toward the playing of music, when I undertook that. I am ready to grant that the artistic performance of fine work may broaden the intelligence and enrich the culture of the man who does it; but never, my lords and gentlemen, the sort of playing that I do.

The Necessary Dash of Bitters

There is not, there never was, any earthly excuse for it except that I like it. But it has had the effect of bringing me around at last to two conclusions, to wit, first, that I shall never understand music, and, second, that I don't give a hoot if it is a mystery to me.

For, once I was relieved of the notion that I could understand it if I worked hard enough, I quit working, whereupon listening to music became merely a pastime and a highly diverting one. I have no patience with those superior persons who are forever denouncing people who regard music as no more than a pleasant sensation in the ears. What's the matter with that? If it is pleasant in the ears, it justifies its existence. But if one has struggled to produce it, it is a great deal pleasanter in the ears when it is well played. Hence struggling to produce it is also justifiable, certainly in the estimation of a frank hedonist.

However, when one has devoted some time to trying to play, certain other matters appertaining to music begin to appear. One is the formidable nature of the difficulties that have to be overcome by an expert, which inevitably heightens the appreciation of a fine performance. A second is some conception of the strange things that have to be done to produce a desired effect, which is the beginning of appreciation of good composition.

Are these, taken together, the rudiments of an understanding of music? Maybe so, but what difference does that make? They are certainly the beginning of something that is interesting and amusing and that may be pursued indefinitely without coming to an end. If the pursuit is attended by defeats that are exasperating, and sometimes maddening, well, what would you have? Do you want to play golf on a course without a single bunker or sand trap? If you do, you are no sport.

In any event, the amateur musician is pretty well insured against the catastrophe of finding the taste of life going flat as he arrives at middle age. However much he may have accomplished, there is always vastly more to be done; however good he is, there is always something that he knows perfectly well how to do and yet can't get done right. Thus there is always in his mixture the dash of bitters requisite to bring out the flavor of the rest.

For my own part, when I have discovered a gold mine in the back yard and have therefore told the boss to take his unfavorably-adjudicated job and go climb a tree, I have a long life's work ready to be entered upon immediately. It is learning to play Debussy's "Syrinx" for flute unaccompanied. It is not the idle dream that one might think, because I come of a conspicuously long-lived family. One grandparent triumphantly reached ninety-two, without playing any musical instrument at all; if the old boy had been equipped with a flute to beguile his later years, who knows what he might have done? At any rate, I if can surpass his achievement by only a few years I may touch the goal. Certainly I shall be extremely busy to the last moment; but "might I of Jove's nectar sup" I should find it no such glorious summation of human existence as, at ninety-six or ninety-eight, at last to play "Syrinx" superbly, take one bow, and let the curtain fall.

A Piano with Dirty Keys

A PIANO WITH DIRTY KEYS

THE 'Cellist, as a housekeeper, does not rank with those fabulous New England women who not only carry out the ashes and clean the hearth, but scrub the fireback after each use of the fireplace. Nevertheless, she has some pride, and for many years it was flicked on the raw every time she glanced at the piano; for the keyboard was, indeed, a dreadful sight to be seen in any household pretending to be civilized. The ivories were not merely smeared, they were grimy; and grimy they remained no matter how many times they were cleaned.

Indeed, they couldn't be cleaned a dozen times a day because our establishment boasts but a single bondwoman, and in these parlous times bondwomen have to be given their due meed of respect or they will walk out on you. Call yours out of the kitchen a dozen, or even half a dozen, times a day to clean the piano keys and see what happens.

So the piano keys went dirty, and the 'Cellist winced, but said nothing. Daily, indeed, she would suggest to the two small Nuisances to whom she and I belong that it is an excellent idea to wash one's hands before sitting down at the piano, but she never made it an iron-clad rule; for, rightly or wrongly, she wanted them to sit down at the piano much more than she wanted an immaculate house.

This was in accordance with a policy deliberately adopted when the Nuisances were very small indeed. The 'Cellist and I are unenlightened parents, reactionary parents, very Bourbons among parents. We are stoutly opposed to allowing the child to express its individuality except, of course, when the expression takes civilized form. We had observed the end results of a policy of enlightenment whereunder the child is permitted to develop his own personality without let or hindrance, and had decided that before we would permit the Nuisances to become such monsters we would take them out and decently drown them. So we have civilized them, sometimes by violence and oppression, but we have civilized them; if we have crushed budding genius by teaching them the difference between *meum* and *tuum*, that is too bad; but we still incline to the belief that what we have really done is keep them from landing in the penitentiary.

A Piano with Dirty Keys

However, from the very beginning we made two exceptions to the general rule that the Nuisances had to learn what was theirs and what wasn't. These two were books and the piano. They have been free to have any book in the house to which they took a fancy from the time when they grew big enough to hold it; and they have been free to pound on the piano to their hearts' content.

As regards the books, this was an exception of no great moment, for our library runs heavily to Everyman and not at all to Elzevir. There are few volumes on the shelves to which grimy hands could do much damage, little that is irreplaceable. But the piano is different. The piano is a really good instrument, much better than any we could afford to buy today. Therefore the sight of its once shining keyboard all streaked and smudged filled the 'Cellist with anxiety, as well as mortification. The more honor to her that she continued to hold her tongue and to keep the piano dissociated, in the minds of the Nuisances, from the inflexible principles of law and order that hedge in life so narrowly.

Those years, however, are gone. The Nuisances are older now, getting into high school age, much too old to go about with grubby paws, and the keys of the piano are relatively clean again.

Moreover, its frame is still solid and stout and its strings can be tuned, so the menace of imminent catastrophe no longer hangs over the house. It is, however, much too early to know definitely whether the 'Cellist and I were wise or foolish. Certain it is that the family includes no young Mozart; probable it is that it has no professional talent; but it has two young people with the ground-work of a musical education.

This has been and continues to be expensive. Music-teachers are among the worst-paid workers in America, but at that they don't work for nothing. A good many hard-earned dollars have gone into this business and a good many more must go into it if it is carried through. The money cost, though, is one of the smallest items in the whole account. What the 'Cellist has put into it in time, physical energy, and nervous strain is beyond all computation. In merely beating time and shouting, "One! Two. Three. Four!" while pudgy fingers fumbled over the keys, I estimate that she has expended enough footpounds of energy to lift the heaviest locomotive on the Baltimore and Ohio Railroad to a height roughly equivalent to the altitude of Mount Washington. In conferences with music-teachers I am sure she has spoken words enough to fill Webster's Unabridged Dictionary three times, while the number of miles she has driven transporting the Nuisances to and from music lessons and concerts is too great even to be guessed.

Nor is that all. The contribution made by the Nuisances themselves is formidable. Even though they have never been chained to the galley, even though they have always known that it was their privilege to quit if that was their deliberate choice, yet many a golden hour have they spent in the music-room when a smiling world was inviting them outside and all sorts of possibilities of delightful play were clamoring for their attention. Many a time, when exercises were too hard and chords and phrases just wouldn't come right, the keys have been further smeared with childish tears. As I grow older, I see more and more clearly that anything purchased at the price of children's tears is a horribly expensive thing. Sometimes the purchase justifies its price, but to do so God knows it must be good!

How good, then, is this thing that the whole family has combined to purchase at such cost? I do not know. Possibly I shall never know. All human calculations are fallible and I am bound to admit the possibility that this one may have been wholly wrong. Still, one can but do one's best with the light that is vouchsafed at the moment, and I understand very clearly the reasoning that has led the 'Cellist and me into this course and that keeps us following it steadfastly.

In the first place, we have no ambition whatever to turn out a pair of professional musicians. This is in part worldly wisdom. Music is both one of the most exacting and one of the worst-paid professions on earth, nor does our observation lead us to believe that professional musicians are conspicuously happier than other people. Let the Nuisances follow what course they will. In the world of the next generation, pretty nearly all paths will be open to women as to men. Let them become astronomers, or gold-beaters, or neurologists, or corporation lawyers; no matter—we are giving them a musical education, anyhow.

In one sense it is the ancient racial obligation that lies upon us. The man who has stood upon his father's shoulders is a poor specimen indeed if he is not willing to bend his back to the weight of his son. Both the 'Cellist and I were given better educations than our fathers had; can we do less than give the Nuisances something better than ours, if it lies within our power to do so? My own schooling, however, included no music, and the 'Cellist's but little; here, then, is an obvious chance to better the record.

A Piano with Dirty Keys

But why music? Why not Esperanto, or thermodynamics, or any of a thousand subjects that neither of us has ever studied?

Well, as we used to say down in North Carolina when a difficult question was posed, that brings on more talk. We have a desire, doubtless sentimental, grounded on folly, perhaps, but none the less strong, to bequeath to our children some legacy of lasting value. Obviously, it will not be money. As for the kind of education that will equip them to fend for themselves in the world, that is less a gift from us to them than the discharge of an obligation laid on us by our fathers, who did as much for us.

What is there, in this chaotic modern world, that a father can leave to his child with a reasonable assurance that it will retain some value always? Certainly not securities—not after 1929. Not material wealth in any form, for our generation has had an almost uniquely impressive lesson in the evanescent nature of the solidly material. Why gold itself, the immemorial wealth of the ages, is now good for nothing except to put into a hole in Kentucky. I would not give the impression that I am scornful of money. On the contrary, I respect it highly, and I wish I could leave some to my children. But no rational man thinks money is the sort of legacy that can never get away from them.

Dismiss the material, then, and consider what intangible values we possess that are worth passing on to the next generation. There is, of course, the inheritance that we are told to prize above rubies, the inestimable treasure of a good name. It is a fine legacy, without doubt, but there is certainly nothing necessarily permanent about it; on the contrary, the child can lose it even faster than he can lose money.

There is religious faith; but he would be bold beyond the point of blasphemy who would arrogate to himself the right to bestow or to withhold this gift.

Beyond that, what is there in the flux of modern life that our generation grips surely enough to be serenely confident of its lasting value? In the economic field, for example, my father held it to be incontestably true, and true without reservation, that thrift is a virtue. I am not so sure. He believed in a system of free competition relieved as far as humanly possible of all artificial restraints, governmental or other. I agree with him in general, but I do not believe that "free" in this connection means what he thought it meant. He believed that "The Wealth of Nations" revealed certain laws of economics comparable, in their universality, to the laws of mathematics; I think that it revealed no more than certain conditional premises, some of which have since been invalidated by changes in the conditions. At all events, I am not prepared to try to instill in the Nuisances any sort of economic faith, confident that it will still hold good fifty years hence.

The uncertainty that has invaded economics is even more pronounced in the realm of politics. I am as yet a stout believer in democratic dogma, but I am bound to admit that it is being sharply and ably challenged. It is no longer inconceivable that the next generation in the United States may have to make shift to survive under some form of totalitarian state. In so far as I have the power, I propose to transmit to my children my own belief in unrestricted liberty wherever it is consistent with social safety, and in the rule of the majority wherever individual liberty is plainly impracticable; but I am far from certain that if I can give them this gift it will retain its value throughout their lives. On the contrary, it may be just the thing that will eventually lead them to end on the barricades or before some *Fuehrer's* firing-squads.

The lesser intangibles that we inherited from the last generation are even more hopelessly confused. Imagine, for example, trying to transmit to the youngsters of today the code of etiquette rigidly maintained by their grandmammas! Imagine wanting to transmit it! Even the foundation of etiquette, the moral code, seems considerably less substantial than it did thirty years ago. Sometime during the long reign of Victoria Regina it appears that decency somehow became separated from honesty and remained apart so long that now when efforts are made to reunite them, one frequently fails to recognize the other, to the confusion of moralists. Nor is it our conception of abstractions only that must be regarded with suspicion; the very cosmos itself has been shaken to pieces. Most certainly I dare not set up any kind of notion of the physical world as beyond debate, when every day some physicist goes a step further toward resolving the whole thing into the shadow of a shade.

Yet there is upon me a strong impulsion to find and present to the youngsters something relatively fixed and stable, if only by way of amends for having brought them into a world so fluid and confusing.

It is one of the heavy penalties of parenthood that from time to time one must stand appalled by what one has done in engendering children. I suppose, in reality, our generation is no worse off in this respect than any other. Perhaps Cro-Magnon Man frequently gazed at Cro-Magnon children with a desperate sense that he had done them wrong in injecting them into a world wherein all the ancient verities were crumbling to a collapse that could not be many years delayed. Perhaps Buck Rogers in the twenty-fifth century will scratch his head over the same problem. Be these things as they may, unquestionably the present generation is face to face with formidable difficulties in this situation.

No thoughtful man escapes it. Heaven knows, my own life has not been the stuff of which high tragedy is made. As I look back over it, I realize that I have been pretty lucky. If fame and fortune have somehow eluded me, Scottish forebears handed down to me an excellent power of adhesion to some kind of pay-roll through fair weather and foul. Even the three great scourges of the race, disease and poverty and war, when they fell upon me, held their hands and whipped but lightly. It is not within reason to suppose that the Nuisances will have an appreciably easier time of it in this world than their father had.

Yet when I look back over that relatively smooth and pleasant path and remember how many thorns and stones were in it, how many laborious ascents under a blazing and pitiless sun, how many dark passages through bitter cold, how many bogs and quagmires, how much pain and fatigue, the thought that the small feet of the Nuisances are destined to tread a path as hard, and perhaps harder, is one on which I do not care to dwell. But it is reason enough for searching high and low, if perchance I may find and put into their hands something that will serve as a staff, however frail, through the long days, or something that in the inevitable gloom of night will be as a lamp unto their feet and a light unto their path.

Will music serve this purpose? I do not know, but I think it may. At any rate, whatever value it has it will retain for a long time unless history alters its course completely. Of course, music, too, has its changes; the old gods go and the new gods arrive in this as in all other arts. Rubinstein fades as Sibelius emerges; and Stravinsky has hardly challenged Sibelius' leadership before Hindemith is challenging his. But behind the rout of household gods there are certain ancient idols, colossi as immovable as Memnon among the shifting sands, and these, I think, will still be colossal when the Nuisances are ancient and gray.

"Put not your trust in princes"—most emphatically not in princes of the present day. Stalin, Mussolini, and Hitler may be great men. There are millions who have staked their very lives on the belief. Yet in the perspective of fifty years they may be as difficult to descry as General Boulanger and Dr. Jameson are today—that is, instead of being regarded as the leaders of immense movements, they may have sunk to the status of slight interruptions of the flow of history. But even if, after half a century, they still occupy each a full page in the encyclopædia, I think that Johann Sebastian Bach will remain a greater personage than all of them put together. Already the Eroica means more in the lives of men than Napoleon the Great does and "Tristan und Isolde" vastly more than Napoleon the Little. In fifty years essentially small men who now loom over the scene because they are close will have sunk out of sight, but I have never a doubt that Händel and Haydn will still be great, that Mozart and Schubert will still have power to stir the hearts of men, and that intimate acquaintance with these giants will still be a solace and a boon.

In this I may be wrong for, as these pages bear abundant evidence, I do not understand music, and the years passed long ago when I was capable of attaining real understanding. For me, therefore,

it is and must ever remain primarily a charming
pastime. Yet ears as dull as mine are capable of
catching hints and intimations, if not the full meaning of the masters. I know that for one who goes
darkling and alone, hag-ridden by

> Ghoulies and ghosties and long leggitit beasties,
> And things that go Whoosh! in the dark,

the thunder of Beethoven is oftentimes a strong
exorcism, hurling back phantoms and scattering
werewolves; I know that for one forspent with the
dust and heat of a weary road there is in the clear,
simple music of old Papa Haydn the sound of cool
water and the shadow of green trees; I know that
on desolate days upon which

> The gray rain beats
> And wraps the wet world in its flying sheets,
> And at my eaves
> A slow wind, ghostlike, comes and grieves and grieves,

there is in the work of Richard Wagner fire and
gold and trumpets, and that lift of the spirit that
raises mortal man to challenge the immortal gods;
and I suspect that even in some of these uncouth
moderns there is a sinewy strength that can help
steady the steps of a traveler dizzied by the whirl-
ing confusion of this century. Perceiving these
things dimly and vaguely, I am persuaded that

with an ear trained to hear them clearly and a mind trained to comprehend them fully, life would have been soothed and softened and rendered more pleasant in a thousand ways.

But this is only half of it, and probably the less important half. Even a half-educated amateur is capable of feeling a response to the stimulus of music, but that is his limit; it is beyond his capacity to evoke that response, because to do that one must play very well indeed. Yet we have it on the highest authority that it is more blessed to give than to receive, and I believe it is as true with regard to music as anything else in life. It doesn't follow that a professional's every appearance is a deep emotional experience, for it is not said that it is more blessed to sell than to receive; but unquestionably a fine musician carries the potential ability to sway others in a fashion beyond the power of the rest of us.

If it would be fine to give to the Nuisances something that will be of value to them, always, would it not be finer yet if it were something that will make them of value to others? I have known selfish musicians; but I have known selfish stockbrokers, too. I do not think the power of music ever developed its possessor into the horseleech's daughter, crying, "Give, Give!" My observation leads me to believe that the tendency is the other way and that the musician who is selfish would have been even more selfish without his training in the art.

At any rate, we like to think, the 'Cellist and I, that the piano with dirty keys has started something that will do more than merely assist the Nuisances themselves along a long weary road. For they will not travel alone, nor will their own adventures be all that will interest them. Even if they escape the misfortune themselves, inevitably they will come upon those who have fallen among thieves and who have been beaten and wounded and left half dead.

Perhaps the day will come when they will find one who is close to them spiritually broken and bleeding. Indeed, in this world, who can doubt that such a day will come? God forbid that they should then act the Priest and the Levite, passing by on the other side. But when all has been done that can be done, and all has been said that can be said, perhaps our gift will furnish them with yet one more resource; perhaps hands once grubby and weak, but strong and sensitive now, will touch a keyboard all white and shining and summon from the realm beyond word and act a spirit to touch the wounds with the touch of oil and wine.

A Piano with Dirty Keys

If it should so happen, then I know it will be with the victim as it was with the wounded man in the old story—from that time forth, he will be Neighbor unto them.

And so the 'Cellist looking at the smudged keys has compressed her lips and said nothing. And so I, ruefully looking over canceled checks returned by the bank—those creased and ink-stained evidences of so much folly, so much stupidity, so much misfortune, such impotence in the clutch of circumstance—find nothing for which to blame myself when I look at those that went to the music-teachers, to the piano-tuners, to the sellers of sheet music and the sellers of concert tickets. And so we sally out together and do fierce and incessant warfare with the schools and acquire the reputation of cranky and probably anti-social parents.

For to accomplish anything worth while in music one must rescue for one's children a minimum of one hour a day for practice; and who can rescue a whole hour of his own child's time from the clutch of the modern school? Even when classes are over, there are athletics and extra-curricular activities; and the parent who dared stand up and declare roundly, "To hell with athletics and all that!" might find himself committed to the lunatic asylum. These things are essential, we are informed with lordly scorn, to developing in the child a social sense, the spirit of give-and-take, the idea of team work.

Then we parents, poor worms that we are, stand and take this rubbish. Granting that outdoor exercise is essential to proper growth, the child doesn't have to take it on a playing-field under the constant instruction and admonition of a hired play-leader. As for social sense, the spirit of give-and-take and the idea of team work, I'll back one hour's playing in a quartet to give the child more of all these than he will get from twenty-four hours' playing on the hockey team.

At any rate, right or wrong, we have done battle ferociously for that hour and propose to carry on. Perhaps this is the last, final proof that we are true amateurs—this determination that our children shall have an opportunity to become something more than rank amateurs, if they have the capacity and the wish to do so.

For the musical amateur is not one to rejoice in his limitations. If he is a wise man, he recognizes them, keeps them ever in mind and makes his course conform to them; that is to say, he accepts them philosophically, which is far from saying that he likes them. If he sees a chance, however, to thrust some one else above his own level of musical competence, he is likely to develop a warm, even fanatical, enthusiasm for the enterprise.

This may be illusion. The supposition is supported by the fact that I have known more than one musician whose high attainments in music command my respect no more than his good sense in other matters, but who exhibits a marked lack of interest in making musicians of his children. Perhaps if I knew more music, I should be less certain of its value. It is the green grass on the other side of the fence.

Yet if the amateur's conception of what it means to be really competent as a musician is illusory, what of it? Life without any illusions at all would be so bleak as probably to be beyond human endurance, and this is one that softens existence without any appreciable enervation of the possessor. At that, it is as likely to be true as any other ideal.

Heaven forfend that I should attempt to set up the thesis that the amateur musician is clear of the foibles and weaknesses that beset the rest of the race. On the contrary, it is just his humanity, his reinforced and emphasized humanity, that makes him a charming fellow. He is too wise to believe that complete disillusionment is either possible or desirable, too realistic to be wholly cynical.

Hence, while he sees with utter clarity the limits of his own ability, and dismisses hope of transcending them, or even of enlarging them to any important extent, he can, and usually does, preserve a childlike faith in the magic of music. His own performance is merely sport, but music is not sport. He may be capable, even at best, of nothing more than sleight-of-hand, but he is confident that, beyond his reach but perceptible, there is a realm of genuine necromancy, inhabited by strong magicians with spells that work.

It is a comforting faith to carry along the road. It means that for the True Believer the road can never come to a dead end, never peter out among sands and cacti. "Man that is born of a woman is of few days, and full of trouble; he cometh forth like a flower, and is cut down." Down, then, we must go; and is it of any marked advantage to go down without a mirage? Is he wise and fortunate who ends in the consciousness only of dust and glare?

I venture to doubt it. I dare to think it is a gracious gift that enables the musician, in the midst of drab confusion, yet to believe in a magic that can bring order and beauty into the world. I count him fortunate, not afflicted, in that he can come to the termination of his journey in the desert, yet with the conviction that although he may go no farther, this is not the end of the road, that though he may never work it, yet there is magic. Deluded your amateur musician may be, but happy he certainly is, because for him the road always goes on, for him, still ahead but in plain sight, there are water and green trees and the mountains of all delight.

THE END